Shadows &
TALL TREES

ISSUE 5
Summer 2013

Editor: Michael Kelly

Copy Editor: Courtney Kelly

UP
UNDERTOW PUBLICATIONS

Shadows & Tall Trees is an annual anthology, open to submissions from August through March. Submissions are assumed to be original and previously unpublished. Please do not query about reprints. Unsolicited manuscripts accepted for publication are paid at 1-cent-per-word to a maximum of $50. Contributors will also receive 2 copies of the journal.

Undertow Publications
Pickering, ON Canada
undertowbooks@gmail.com

www.undertowbooks.com

CONTENTS

EDITOR'S NOTE

When I started publishing Shadows & Tall Trees I told myself I'd publish 5 issues and then re-evaluate its status. Thus, issue 5, which you hold in your hands, is the last issue to be printed in its present incarnation. Instead, from issue 6 onward, the format will change to a yearly trade-paperback anthology and eBook.

There are myriad reasons for this change.

When reading submissions, there are always a number of excellent stories that I have to turn down because they don't quite fit the journal's aesthetic. By widening the journal's purview, I can include some of these excellent stories. My focus will still be the weird and dark, but I'll be able to publish some of the odd, unclassifiable stories that come my way. As well, I'd like to include more non-fiction; specifically essays, criticism, and interviews.

I'd envisioned the magazine as an old-school literary journal. A niche, craft product. In that regard, an eBook wasn't in my plans. A change to a yearly anthology necessitates some new thinking. So, for those who were asking, I will make it available in digital form.

With this change, subscriptions to the journal will cease. Postage rates have made the subscription model impossible to sustain. Economically, a yearly anthology is much more viable and feasible.

So, future volumes of Shadows & Tall Trees promise to be bigger and better than ever.

Many thanks for your continued support.

Michael Kelly
June, 2013

NEW WAVE

Gary Fry

Jacob, in his singsong way, said, "Daddy, poo, stinks, needs wash."

"Don't talk such nonsense," replied Lee, responding to his son's words without too much concern. This was what seven year-olds were like, after all; it was perfectly normal. But after a day at the computer correcting distance-learning students' manuscripts, Lee now had all the housework to attend to and could do without any reminders of the past.

"Isn't it time you were going to bed?" he asked Jacob, running the vac around his feet in the lounge. The boy was playing on his Xbox, an activity that, Lee's academic reading had taught him, was less damaging than tabloid headline writers claimed. "Or do you want some supper first?"

"Got a bellyache," Jacob replied, dropping his plastic controller and then clutching his guts.

Lee looked at him warily, turning off the vac so he no longer had to raise his voice. The boy wouldn't start at his new school till next month, and had no reason to feign illness in the way that had always annoyed Jane. But Lee kept his mind off all that. This wasn't the first time lately that his son had complained of minor ailments. Lee wondered whether he should take him to see the doctor with whom they'd just registered, after moving into the area. It might be wise putting faces to their names with the medic.

"Okay, finish your game and then get some sleep. You're sure to feel better in the morning."

"It's not even dark yet, Daddy."

That was true: the countryside through the uncurtained lounge window was alive with dwindling May sunlight. But a sneaky wind gusted; Lee heard it feeling furtively under the bungalow's eaves, like someone else present in the building.

But he shut off that thought, too.

Later, once he'd put his son to bed with a kiss, Lee returned to the lounge and stared out of the same window. When he'd first viewed the property, the field at the rear (it belonged to a farmer who lived further along the lane, apparently) had been cropped close to the ground. Now this had altered, with knee-high wheat waving like armies at combat. It was difficult to tell whether the movement was an effect of clouds moving across a restless sky, filleting sunlight into delicate hues, or rather multiple winds crisscrossing the area. Maybe it was both. Whatever the truth was, Lee found it difficult to continue observing.

He retreated to the kitchen for a sandwich and a glass of beer, trying to forget how much like a churning body of water the field of wheat looked.

≈≈

The following morning, Jacob's stomach ailment had vanished; he ate a full bowl of Weetabix followed by toast with butter and jam. Lee was relieved to see the boy's appetite return, and despite all his scientific training, he clung rigidly to a housewives' tale that if a person was eating heartily, there could be little wrong with him or her.

After breakfast, Jacob got dressed and then approached his daddy working at the PC in their spare room downstairs.

"Can I go and play out now?"

A trickle of fear scurried through Lee's guts, like toxins he'd been forced to swallow. But then he realized that nothing could threaten the boy here. There was just flat land and, other than the farmer, nobody living within a mile to the nearby village. That had been its appeal, of course, after their move from the coast earlier in the year.

"Yes, of course," Lee replied, his eyes averted and looking at a single icon in the margin of his monitor screen: PHOTOS, it was called. He knew it dated back years, from before his son was born. Lee had simply forgotten to consign it to the bowels of the machine. "But don't go too far. And…" A pause as words clotted in his throat, like too much water seeking to pass through a bottleneck. But then he finished, "And be careful."

"I will!" Jacob said, but as was a boy's wont, he was halfway out of the house already. Lee recalled his own childhood and energetic habits; he'd scared his mother half to death a lot of the time.

After hearing the front door shut with a slam, Lee tried returning to his work—hell, some of his students needed a serious reality check about academic standards—but soon found himself seeking to activate that icon in the screen's margin. Every part of him rebelled against opening what he knew would cause him grief, but it wasn't long before complex emotions prompted the action: he clicked to open the folder, bracing himself for impact.

Here was Jane looking regal as ever, her straw-blond hair flowing in a summer breeze. They'd taken their first trip to the coastal town in which they'd ended up living, and in this snap, her face appeared relatively unmarked by the thoughts that would trouble her following the birth of Jacob. The following shots showed their beautiful boy, as an infant and then a toddler and finally a robust four year old…just before Jane had…

But Lee quickly shut the folder.

There was no use dwelling on all that had happened. He supposed fate was storing up complications for later life—despite taking the news well, Jacob would one day suffer from having no mother now—but it would be foolish to offer these a facilitating hand. No, better to press down, holding them below the surface. They might even drown down there; that certainly happened.

≈≈

Jacob returned safely for lunch, and after his adventures in their new neighbourhood, he ate well, sandwich after sandwich. He told his daddy that he'd found a den, but refused to reveal where this was, because it was a secret. Lee felt a little uneasy about that, but again tuned into his own youth and realized that such privacy was also just an ordinary aspect of childhood, and certainly nothing like Jane's furtiveness had become.

When the boy went out again later that afternoon, Lee issued strict instructions to return before seven and then took a beer—a local brew he'd bought in the village—into the lounge to sit looking at the field, waving like an imperious sea.

After what had happened to his late wife, to Jacob's mother, this interpretation troubled him, but short of asking the farmer to cut the wheat before it reached full crop, he'd have to get used to it. The last thing he wanted was to sour relations with new neighbours. Jane's erratic behaviour had led to enough of that in their previous home and was one of the reasons why Lee had desired a clean break following her death.

The field of wheat waved back and forth, forming hypnotic patterns in Lee's mind as moody clouds rolled overhead. With alcohol in his blood, he grew transfixed, as if elements of the swaying crop were taking on more life than they should, clustering like grassy knots and stealing towards him with whispering haste. But after blinking and looking again, he saw nothing more than wheat lashing to and fro, like waves on a fretful body of water tossed by mysterious gravitational forces. It must be a light shower that lent the field such a washed-out, wriggling texture.

It would be alarming if he started to hallucinate. Jacob surely had enough biological material to handle without Lee also handing on a fragile set of genes. But such reductionist accounts of schizophrenia had been discredited, hadn't they? Despite training in sociology, Lee knew the field well. He'd done much research on mental illness when Jane had been diagnosed months after their son was born. Lee was no expert, but felt confident that a physiological link between parent sufferers and their offspring was tenuous at best. Social exposure and learning had as much to do with it. But Jane was now gone. Jacob had nothing more to fear.

Lee, wiping tears from his eyes, sat watching the waving field of wheat until his son came home from his newfound adventures.

≈≈

The boy looked soaking wet upon entering the house.

"How on earth did you get like that?" Lee wanted to know, his anger surely disproportionate to whatever his son had been up to. "Did you find a pond? And did you fall in?"

Jacob looked puzzled by his daddy's raised voice, to such a degree that he cowered while replying. "No, it was just the field. The grass is *this* high..."—he put a hand up to his shoulders—"...and now it's all covered in rain."

Was that true? Had gathering clouds brought down enough water to soak the boy's clothes like this? Lee took his son upstairs and helped him remove his T-shirt and pants. And then his concerns were replaced by a more serious one: Jacob's whole body was covered in a rash.

Red wheals ran over his arms, down his back, and along the front of his legs. These marks looked sore and were interspersed by many violent pimples full of yellowish pus. Lee was loath to touch the things, but after helping his son take a shower, he rubbed calamine lotion onto the affected skin before putting him to bed.

They'd have to visit the doctor's tomorrow; while washing, the boy had said his flesh felt "all itchy and ucky and horrid." That was the kind of mangled language Jane had often deployed, and Lee's fear was worsened by Jacob's final comment before Lee shut his bedroom door: "I wish Mummy was here to make it better."

≈≈

In the middle of the night, Lee was awoken by screaming —by no means the only time this had occurred in the last six or seven years. The noise was high-pitched and fretful, but on this occasion not directly beside him, not from the person who shared his bed. It was coming from the next

11

room, its hysterical quality belonging to a child rather than a woman.

Lee got up at once and rushed through to his son's bedroom. This one looked onto the rear of the property — onto that wet, waving field – though the curtains were tugged tightly together, rendering the bed an insidious white block in the blackness all around. The boy was thrashing in the sheets, as if someone lay with him, but when Lee's fumbling fingers eventually found the light switch, the dark retreated behind the furniture, twitching like restless shadows.

Then Lee reached the bed.

"Jacob! Jacob! What's wrong?"

The boy glanced up from his pillow, his face little more than a pale mask. In the plunging V of his pyjama's neckline, Lee could see the rash still emblazoned on his chest. Had the itchy discomfort woken him? But how to account for his frantic limbs, which ceased moving only after Lee pinned them down?

"Jacob...Jacob...look at me. It's your daddy. You're safe. Everything's okay."

But was that true? His son's eyes looked glossy and vague, the pupils dilated as if he was under the influence of powerful medication. Lee tried not to recall the effect that anti-psychotic drugs had had on his late wife, focusing instead on the problem at hand: his son surely on the verge of hyperventilation.

After Lee had hugged the boy, like the under-protected infant he'd once been, Jacob finally adjusted to reality: his harmless new room in a harmless new locale. The quiet hereabouts testified to these facts, though Lee was disturbed to realize that it wasn't absolute silent, after all: he could hear wheat waving in a soft breeze, like desperate whispers from the throat of someone suffocating.

Or *drowning*, he reflected, trying hard not to interpret the sounds from that field as the gentle susurration of a distant sea.

But now he had his son to deal with.

"Jacob, what scared you? Is it another bellyache? Is it the rash?"

Lee recalled that Jane had suffered skin disorders,

especially during the time of her breakdown, but this wasn't grounds for concern. Some inherited ailments were less than pernicious, surely. Lee himself suffered periodic eczema acquired from his father's side of the family; this was hardly life-threatening. More to the point, it was far from *self*-threatening.

"I had...I had..." Jacob began to reply, dry-swallowing irrepressible sobs, "I had a *nightmare*, Daddy. A *nasty* nightmare."

"And...what was it about, son?"

Lee wasn't sure he wanted to know, but Jacob seemed intent on telling him. Family duties could be relentless; Lee had certainly learnt that over the last few years. And a man's obligations involved managing horrors for those he loved: a wife's, a child's... Surely he could now get one of them right.

The boy said, "It was about a person out in that field behind our house. But its body was bent all funny. It looked like it was waving at me. Then it started moving. Its upper half was folded over, but I couldn't see how its legs could fit, because the hard ground was where they should be. It was sitting up, but seemed to...drift my way through all the grassy stalks. Its arms swung forwards over its head, one after the other, like it was...it was..."

Swimming, Lee thought with unease, but didn't say aloud. All he could see in his mind's eye was a flopping, boneless figure struggling towards the house, performing an inexpert front-crawl across that churning sea of wheat.

Then his son added, "Its arms and face were...falling apart, Daddy. And it had long, wet hair."

"Like a...girl's?" Lee asked, the question escaping with needful haste.

"No," the boy replied, and this at least comforted his father...until Jacob finished, "Like a *woman's.*"

≈≈

The source of the boy's nightmare became apparent the following day: the farmer who owned the land at the back of the house had placed a scarecrow at the heart of the field in which the frightful apparition had appeared.

Over a breakfast of toast and cereal, Lee told his son

that he'd probably seen the framework for the straw-stuffed figure yesterday, while exploring the area. He might also have spotted the scarecrow being prepared at the farm down the lane.

"But, Daddy, I *didn't*," Jacob protested in a plaintive voice. But Lee refused to accept this, drawing on ideas from his academic discipline to lend his interpretation authority.

"We sometimes see things we don't acknowledge, son," he explained, trying not to examine the sore patches on the boy's arms. "But our brains recall these while we sleep, piecing them together like a crazy...I mean, like a silly film."

Lee sometimes thought this was what the visions of schizophrenia must be like, but experienced while conscious. Some of the things Jane had described during bad episodes had frightened him as much as Jacob's description had last night. Dreadful creatures had tried entering their home, his late wife had claimed. She'd also commonly imagined that everyone around her was plotting to drown her. Maybe *that* fantasy had arisen from living close to the sea.

But Lee should consider all this later. Right now, he had to take his son to the doctor's.

After encouraging the boy to wash down his food with a glass of barley water, Lee went to the lounge to fetch his car keys from the coffee table. He knew he could no longer postpone reflection on what had happened before their move inland, but at the moment he had more practical matters to attend to.

He glanced again through the lounge's window, at that waving sea of wheat – the farmer's field. The scarecrow at the centre glared back, its baleful stillness unnerving. A breeze whistled through its ragged eye sockets, making a sound like uneasy whispering. Its straw hair lolled with no more enthusiasm than its misshapen limbs.

≈≈

"Could you tell me what Jacob's diet consists of?"

The doctor was an attractive woman about Lee's age,

though it was too early to be thinking about courtship. Nevertheless, he'd noticed that there was no ring on her third-left finger and that her smile lingered whenever their eyes met... But he was supposed to be focusing on his son's ailment.

Lee explained that the boy liked sandwiches, toast and breakfast cereal. Each item elicited a nod from the doctor, who'd already examined Jacob's chest and arms. Once Lee finished, the woman typed notes into her electronic file, before turning to the boy and his father to propose a diagnosis.

"We'll need to arrange some tests, but from the symptoms you've described—bellyaches and all these nasty sores..."

"My bones sometimes ache, too," Jacob added, clearly proud to have spoken up in public; he was often shy with strangers and tended to withdraw from social encounters, just as his mother had.

"That is also consistent with what I have in mind," the doctor added, smiling again as she returned her gaze to Lee.

But Lee was examining his son. "You never mentioned aching bones, Jacob," he said, as if the words were a private rebuke only the two of them could appreciate, a family code so secret nobody else had access to it. Then Lee glanced back at the doctor and asked, "So what's wrong with him? Forgive my terseness. I'm a little anxious."

"Of course you must be," the doctor replied, and if she'd already read the family's notes, she'd be aware of sensitivities about the boy's health. "Nevertheless, you shouldn't worry unduly. I think your son is suffering from *celiac disease*. It's a condition that damages the small intestine and prevents it from absorbing parts of food that are important to remain healthy. The problem is caused by an adverse reaction to gluten, which is found in barley, rye, and wheat. That is why Jacob's beloved sandwiches, toast and cereal have led to an outbreak of symptoms."

Lee was half-relieved to hear that his son's condition appeared to be a food allergy, presumably treatable by modifying his diet. Nevertheless, the doctor's reference to 'wheat' had disturbed him, making him remember all the

15

boy had said after waking overnight with a scream. Lee's hands shook as he took Jacob protectively in his arms.

After the doctor had explained a little more about the condition and how it could be dealt with, she arranged for tests to be conducted in the nearest hospital, thirty miles from the village. Lee presently had no transport, having sold his previous car after getting a job with the online college. But they could make the journey by bus, of course. He thanked the doctor and made sure Jacob did the same before they stepped out of the surgery, into a brooding spring afternoon.

It looked as if a storm was on its way.

≈≈

That night, after several hours spent playing in the front garden, Jacob experienced the dream again. Lee went to him in the same way, comforting with more bullshit from his academic discipline. Lee believed little of this, even as it spilled automatically from his mouth. Hadn't he tried similar desperate strategies with Jane? His late wife, also educated, had dismissed his approach as "intellectual imperialism", while simultaneously complaining about foes lurking in their cellar, on the roof, in her bedroom.

The boy had no such defence, of course, but nonetheless went on about a figure with "shadow for eyes" and "skin that looks like mine, but mostly fallen off." Lee told himself this was just a nightmare, but was so tired after the previous night's disruption that reason squirmed from his grasp and he stepped across to the boy's window, flung apart the curtains and looked outside into a motionless night.

There was nothing in the field but darkness, but in a nebulous area, where the land met the sky, a small shape was visible, ragged-edged and flanked by the wavering horizon.

This was just the scarecrow standing in its field of wheat, Lee decided, even though his mind now felt infected by demons from the past. His son was unaware of what had happened on the coast—everybody was, even the police. This was something Lee must confront before long, and as he settled Jacob again for sleep—the boy protested with garbled language, which did little to inspire Lee's confidence—the world around their new home stirred like a restless sea.

≈≈

Lee was unsure what he'd say once they reached the farm, but he'd recently dealt with worse situations and felt confident in his ability to improvise. He and Jacob had taken a walk along the lane to the village after breakfast —no bread or cereal this time, just fresh fruit and yogurt —and after reaching a collection of old barns and buildings, they listened to the bleating of cattle and sheep.

"I like animals," the boy said, rubbing one leg as if it was painful. Lee told himself that his son had probably pulled a muscle while playing out the other day, rather than the bone inside aching. After all, that was what Jane, the boy's mother, had often complained about while suffering schizophrenic episodes.

"We can walk back across the fields, if you like," Lee replied, keen to reach the farmer's residential dwelling. "If we find a horse, we can stroke it."

The prospect cheered Jacob, who took his daddy's hand as they advanced further into the muddy farmyard.

The farmer when he appeared was taciturn in appearance, with weather-worn hands and a firm walk. He carried two buckets, and dark stuff inside splashed against his legs as he crossed to a barn. After spotting the newcomers, he appeared far from unwelcoming, yet nonetheless wary. Maybe he thought Lee looked like an official—a tax inspector or a farming regulator—but surely having Jacob beside him mitigated any threat.

"Can I help you?" asked the farmer, his voice warm and deep, like a fondly regarded uncle or grandfather.

Lee, holding his son's hand, explained that they'd recently moved into the house along the road. He kept his words ambiguous about the presence of a wife and mother, wanting to avoid the inevitable conversation.

By this time, a woman had emerged from the farmhouse nearby. She was a similar age to her husband, late-fifties, and looked a little too fond of home-grown produce. While waddling across, her eyes never left Jacob and she wore a smile that, for some reason, Lee interpreted as the exclusive domain of those denied children of their own.

"Oh, Mr Baker," the woman said with mock seriousness, her gaze flitting temporarily to the farmer, "you failed to let your good wife know that we had such a handsome guest."

Jacob smiled in response to the hand the woman laid on his head, and then Lee judged it a perfect moment to deal with his difficulty.

"I'm afraid I'm about to be a pest," he began, looking at the couple the woman had just revealed in a playful way as the Bakers. "My son Jacob hasn't been sleeping well these last few nights. I'm sorry to say that he's developed a bit of a...well, a *phobia*, I guess you'd call it...involving the scarecrow you've placed near our home."

"No, Daddy, *she* isn't a scarecr—"

"Let me deal with this, son," Lee interrupted, and after looking again at the farmer, he added, "Do you see my problem here?"

"You want me to take the scarecrow down?" the man asked, his brow furrowing. Compassion and the necessity of earning a living fought for supremacy in his unblinking gaze. "That field's worth quite a lot to me, my friend..."

"The name's *Lee*."

"Good to meet you, Lee. But all the same, if I don't have something frightful standing there, to scare away those greedy buggers, the wheat'll be ruined."

And far from a bad thing, given all the damage it causes, Lee reflected, but avoided saying aloud, even though his anxieties tempted him to do so.

"I understand that," he eventually replied, his mind slipping like a collapse of earth during some natural catastrophe. "But I was hoping that maybe, until we're settled in, and after Jacob here..."—he ruffled his son's hair—"...has got used to the area...well, I was hoping you could maybe make the scarecrow a little less..." — another hesitation, during which creepy thoughts stole across Lee's psyche. But then he finished, "...I was hoping you could make it a little less *lifelike*."

"Lifelike?" the farmer said, his face registering

18

bewilderment.

Ragged holes for eyes…slipshod limbs…a shambling figure that bent at the middle and then swam across the field…

Lee realized how absurd his request must sound and thought it was now time to leave. At least he'd asked politely, and not issued the irascible demands his late wife had used to legitimize her delusions. Neighbours on the coast had been less than understanding, but Lee hoped the Bakers would appreciate his difficulty with the boy. Hell, they might even guess that his son had no mother, that Lee's wife was dead.

After bidding an awkward farewell, Lee began walking towards the farm's exit, tugging Jacob by the hand as the boy said in a private whisper, "Daddy, I told you, it's not the *scarecrow* I'm scared of. It's a *wom*—"

But that was when a voice spoke from behind. It was Mrs Baker, whom Lee had decided had no offspring of her own.

"Be sure to bring your boy into the village each weekend. We have lots of activities for youngsters. There's Cub Scouts, sports clubs, and swimming up at the school."

Swimming, thought Lee, as if caught in the eye of the storm gathering overhead. Then he felt his mind collapse like a building swept away by a thunderous sea.

≈≈

He hadn't meant to kill his wife; this had merely been an improvisation.

Lee had put his son to bed an hour earlier and now sat in the lounge in front of his laptop. He'd had several beers—the local brew he'd bought from a village store, one with plenty of wheat in it—and the alcohol facilitated recollections of the previous year's events.

Jane had been convinced that a tragedy would befall her, almost certainly involving the sea she'd been able to observe from their property's windows. She'd believed that someone—a neighbour, one of the few close friends her condition hadn't driven away, or even Lee or Jacob—would submerge her in water.

Lee had grown exasperated, and after the failure of higher dosages of medication, had decided to take

19

practical steps unapproved by her specialist. He'd hired a boat to take her out to sea with every intention of teaching his wife to swim.

It had been a stormy day, with few other sailors, amateur or otherwise, straying far from the coastline. Jane had been suffering a mild spell at the time, her paranoia and jumbled communications at a minimum. Lee was under strain, having worried for months about how his wife's episodes would impact on their son. Jacob seemed robust and unaware of his mother's behaviour, but how long would that last? After attending school and realizing that other children's parents were not the same, would he suffer damage then?

Jane had insisted on taking a swimming lesson away from other people; she'd never liked doing anything in public, even with a disinterested audience. The cranky weather had rendered the sea ice-cold, but Jane's condition resulted in variable body temperatures, and she didn't suffer the way others did. For the sake of his wife and child, Lee had endured this.

Choppy waves had compromised his attempt to demonstrate the breaststroke. Once in the sea, he'd kept his arms around his wife until they were a good distance from the boat. Then he'd set her free, encouraging her to use her arms and legs to propel herself towards him, now twenty yards away.

Perhaps he should have tried harder. Maybe they should have conducted the lesson in shallow water and less inclement weather. But Jane rarely perceived danger in common acts. Lee had observed her for years and had realized how willing she was to carry out certain activities —particularly those that might lead to a diminution of threat—in risky circumstances.

But he was surely ascribing retrospective motivations to his behaviour that day. He *hadn't* killed her. The crashing sea had simply swept her away, a terrible tragedy. That was what the police had believed, anyway. Lee had been genuinely remorseful, recalling his wife's bobbing straw-blond hair as her arms flailed in the tossing water. And if any aspect of him *had* plotted her demise—the furtive subconscious, where demons lurked —he could surely excuse himself by claiming that he'd done it for his son, for innocent Jacob, who shared with his mother half his genes and would struggle to get by even without her interference.

Wheat, thought Lee, now half-drunk. Glancing up through the lounge window of his new inland home, he saw that field swaying back and forth like a restless sea. The storm growing in the sky was a twisted facsimile of the one that had blighted that terrible day last year. But he mustn't think about that any more. He ought to focus only on the future. There was one thing he'd pledged to do as soon as possible: scour the internet for information about the impact of wheat on a celiac disease sufferer.

Feeling observed—that was just the hideous scarecrow at a reassuring distance; the farmer had yet to replace it with something less unsightly—Lee typed a few words into his laptop's search engine and, seconds later, was rewarded with a list of websites. Most looked medical, with bullet-pointed lists of symptoms and treatments. But then his gaze chanced upon a chilling word: *schizophrenia*.

Lee accessed this site and soon found himself reading a speculative essay by an American scientist who'd tried to establish a link between the consumption of wheat and this mental health condition. Apparently in studies conducted in the 1960s, experts had found that the prevalence of celiac disease in schizophrenics was 50 to 100 times higher than could be expected by chance. Similarly, celiac doctors had observed that their patients were ten times more likely to suffer schizophrenia than the general population. In short, gluten—a substance found in foodstuff such as rye, barley and wheat—was poisonous to certain people, including sufferers of celiac disease…

Lee looked up.

The scarecrow on the horizon, across that sea of waving wheat, had begun to move. The wind was now stronger as the storm got underway, twitching the jerry-built head of the thing, with its straw-blond hair and slipshod musculature.

≈≈

The next Lee knew he was being shaken awake by tiny hands. He jerked up, his head heavy with all the beer he'd consumed the previous evening. The light around him felt stark and invasive, but not as much as the hysterical voice he now heard, which reminded him of many fretful mornings in his past.

"*Daddy, she's coming! She's coming now!*" his son cried, shaking him again by one arm.

"Who...what...?" replied Lee, swiping his free arm across his face until his vision was cleared of sticky nocturnal residue.

Then he looked up ahead, to where Jacob's other arm pointed.

The field beyond their home was a tossing sea of makeshift waves, its wheat swept to and fro by savage winds and rain lashing down with saturating force. Although vision beyond a hundred yards was compromised, Lee thought he saw a shape at the far end of the field, a dark cross set against the restless sky. The scarecrow's perch was no longer tenanted, leading Lee to assume that the farmer had agreed to his plaintive request. But then he recalled what his son had said, and looked a little lower.

The figure flopping through the wet wheat was little more than a fragmenting husk, its straw-like hair wrapped around a face as patchy as stained sackcloth. Only its upper body could be observed, jerking and reeling above the bogus sea's surface. The arms, impossibly bent like the torso was, made a forlorn attempt to swim as the whole figure struggled in the storm.

"It's...just the sc-scarecrow," Lee said, his voice stammering with panic. He no longer knew whether he was trying to reassure his son or himself. "The wind has b-blown it off its stand, that's all. And now it's being p-pushed this way."

"No, Daddy, n—" Jacob began, but got no further. Lee had hushed him with a hand over his mouth. With the other, he roused the laptop and accessed an electoral-role website. He typed in the name 'Baker' and then that of the village nearby. Only three entries were returned, one surely the contact details of the couple further along the lane. Lee snatched up the telephone from the sideboard and made the call.

It was the woman who answered.

"Hello?" she said, and then Lee launched into his attack.

It was fear that informed his words; he threatened his new neighbours with legal action if they did nothing about the meddlesome scarecrow he'd asked them to remove. Although Jacob had kept his eyes fixed on the ragged figure with shadowy eyes thrashing through the field, the boy seemed disturbed to see his daddy lapse into a paranoiac frenzy.

"I'm sorry you feel that way, my dear, but there must be some mistake," Mrs Baker replied, but went silent for a moment, prompting Lee's gaze to return to the flopping thing getting closer to his new home. It possessed little by way of a mouth, just a dark slit full of dirt. Then the woman added, "My husband removed the scarecrow first thing this morning, before the storm arrived. Neither of us could bear the look of fear in your son's eyes yesterday. We...just wanted to help."

Daddy, I told you, it's not the scarecrow I'm scared of, Lee heard Jacob say deep in his mind, where all the darkest material stirred at times of duress. Then he dropped the phone, went across to the boy to hold him, and glanced out at the ragged shape still struggling through that tempestuous sea of wheat.

And for the first time since the terrible event had occurred, Lee was glad he'd never got around to teaching his late wife to swim.

CASTING AMMONITES

Claire Massey

She arrived just as a gull lifted from the sea—sprung from the tip of a wave, it did, salt frosting its sodden feathers. She was unexpected. I didn't see her stumble down the path, or linger peering into the huts, the way people do, as though no one lives here. Happen it's them wearing the place away with all their gawping, with all the pictures they take.

It was lip-splitting cold. One of those mornings when the dark clings to the edges of the sky, waiting to rush back in. The light was stretched out thin across everything. I'd taken the boat out to drop the pots first thing. Baited them with mackerel. Left a constellation of buoys in the black water, a snare of ropes underneath. I lit a fire, but I can never get warm once the sea's touched my bones. In winter, if I sit here long enough I'm sure I'll turn to stone. Be some fossil hunter's prize discovery. They'll put me in the Whitby museum.

She was right on the cusp of the sea. Hadn't stopped to look at the rocks, to pick them up and feel the weight of years in them, to unclasp her fingers hoping to find curls of time in her palms. People only come here to take the stones. After a while, she took a step back from the sea, and then another. She had an old satchel, and from it she pulled out a sketch book and pencil—she'd come to take something after all. When the wind stripped the hair from her face I realized she was older than I'd thought. But it was only later, close to, I could see the lines round her eyes that outlasted her smile and the wiry grey curls budding in her dark hair.

I let her find me. She crouched on the sea-slick stones. Dipped her fingers into pools to retrieve skeletal seaweed and held it up, dripping, against the sky. She fingered stones but she didn't hammer them or try to split them apart like so many do. She didn't draw anything. She was putting the sketch book back into her satchel when she looked up and saw me. She turned away, back to the line of sea and sky. But she knew she was being watched. Her movements became more considered. She tried to keep her back to me.

It was the labyrinth that caught her. She half-skipped with delight, self-consciousness shed. Most who walk the beach don't find it. The stones are shrouded in seaweed. Their pattern has to be felt through the soles as much as seen. Once she'd recognized it she walked around it rather than into it. Clever girl.

When the coil of stones was between us she looked up and right at me. The wind had taken up so much of her hair it seemed she was suspended from the sky. She wound back round the edge of the circle towards me.

Hello, she said, when she was close enough that I might hear her over the water.

Hello, I said, beckoning for her to come and sit beside me on the bench. People always wonder at there being furniture down here, can't believe it was carried down the steep cliff path. Most of it wasn't. I'm waiting for a piano to wash up with the tide, crusted with so much salt and rust you have to crack its strings to get a note from it.

She sat, dragged her hair back from the wind's reach and accepted the glass I'd been cradling. My best glass. Etched with sea air. Whisky tastes better from that than anything. Even the cheap stuff.

Thank you, she said. Her voice cracked with cold and maybe a little with sadness. I couldn't be sure.

You didn't draw anything, I said. You did right. It's better that way.

She took a sip of the whisky and let an ammonite fall from her hand to her lap. They're unsettling, she said, the stones.

They're snakestones, I said.

I was pleased she hadn't called them beautiful. They're not beautiful, these tight old knots of dead stone.

It's St. Hilda's work, I said. The woman transformed a plague of snakes. There used to be a good trade in carving heads on them. Some people will do anything to make a story true.

I took the stone from her lap and ran my finger along the cold outer ridges of the whorl. No one knows what they looked like, I told her. The soft part, the outline of the body, never survived in stone. An ammonite lived in the mouth of its shell, built itself room after room as it grew, sealing each one off behind it.

So it could never go back.

No, it could never go back.

She drained the whisky. That made me smile, though I was glad I hadn't got out the good stuff.

Could I draw you? She looked away as she asked, already expecting my answer.

No, no, none of that. I'd probably turn to dust. Be nothing but pencil lines on the breeze. You've got to be careful who you let catch you.

You don't remember me, do you?

I wasn't expecting that. I searched her face, the turn at the corner of her mouth. The light blue eyes—irises so pale they were in danger of slipping into the whites. No, I don't know you, I said.

I took the glass and refilled it from the bottle I keep propped between stones under the bench.

Your hut's being eaten by rust, she said.

It's growing another skin.

I let my head rest back against the familiar grooves of metal. We sat with nothing else to say and everything unsaid, and passed the glass between us. Minutes swelled. The sea slowed till it barely touched the shore. The moment stretched right out to its bare bones and I felt warmth sink into me. The crack was almost imperceptible, but she roused and took back the ammonite she'd collected. Cast it onto the beach. The tide returned to take it.

Did you make the labyrinth?

No, it was here before I came. It's for catching trolls, bad winds, spirits. Fishermen have made them for centuries. Not so much now, perhaps.

Have you walked it?   No. I tend it. Watch over it.

What happens if I walk into it? she asked. Do you lose me again?

I don't know you. I'm sorry.

I didn't know what else to say. She was on her feet, stumbling across stones fresh-licked by spray. If I could have tied her down with ropes I would. Come back, I shouted, but I was spitting into the wind. She followed the bight of the labyrinth, wound her way into it, right to the centre. For a breath, her defiance held back the rush of the tide. I did remember her. But already there's silt and saltwater collecting around her feet. There was a woman, a girl.

What was I telling you?

A CAVERN
OF REDBRICK

Richard Gavin

See now as the boy sees. Bear witness to a summerworld, a place sparkling with clear light and redolent with the fragrance of new-mown grass and where the air itself hosts all the warmth and weightlessness of bathwater.

It is the first morning in this summerworld and, knowing that autumn is but a pinpoint in the future, Michael stands on the porch of his grandparents' country home and allows the elation to erupt inside him. He then mounts his bicycle and rides headlong into the season.

The town whisks past him in a verdant smear. But Michael holds his destination firmly in his mind's eye.

The gravel pit on the edge of town has long been his private sanctuary. He has escaped to that secret grey place more times than he can possibly remember. It is his own summer retreat, one of the many highlights of spending the summer with his grandparents in the little village of Cherring Point.

Visiting the pits is technically trespassing; his grandfather, who is charged by the government to occasionally man and maintain the place, has often told him to keep away from it. Thus Michael keeps his mild transgressions to himself. Clearly he isn't the only one to sneak into the secluded area. He isn't the one who has cut the hole into the chain-link fence that distinguishes the property line, though he *does* always make sure to recover this portal with the brush that camouflages it.

Michael consoles himself with the logic that he really never disrupts anything in the pits. On his bike he would race over the mounds, which he likes to imagine as being the burial sites of behemoths. He loves watching his tires summon dirty fumes of gravel dust. Often that instant when his bike soars past the tipping point at the mounds' summit, Michael feels as though he is flying.

It is his private ritual of summer elation; harmless and pure.

Except that today, on his inaugural visit of the season, Michael discovers that his ritual ground is no longer private...

His initial reaction to seeing the girl beyond the fence is shock, a feeling that gives way to an almost dizzying sense of disbelief.

At the far end of the lot is a large redbrick storage shed, its door of corrugated metal shut firm and secured with a shiny silver padlock. Michael has often fantasized about all manner of treasure being stored within those walls.

Standing on the shed's roof is a girl whom Michael guesses to be no older than he is. She is dressed in a t-shirt only slightly whiter than her teeth. Her straw-coloured hair hangs to the middle of her back. Her bare feet are uncannily balanced at the very summit of the shed's pitched roof, yet she does not teeter or wave her arms to maintain this daring balance. She is as stationary as a totem.

Michael can feel her eyes upon him.

He veers his bike away and rides the paths above the gravel yard for a while, cutting sloppy figure-eights in the dirt while wrestling with whether or not he should retreat. What exactly is she trying to prove standing on the shed that way? What if she tries to speak to him, to suss out his reasons for coming here? What if this place is in fact *her* special place? Perhaps *he* has been the real outlander all this time.

Michael veers his bike cautiously back to the hidden gap in the fence, hoping, foolishly, that the girl will flee. He crouches low on his bike and glides to where the brush is thickest.

"What's your name?"

The sound of her voice chills Michael. He wonders how she has spied him. Does her position on the roof make her all-seeing?

Like a surrendering soldier, Michael rides out from behind the greenery, clears the entrance to the pits and eases his back toward the shed.

"How did you get up there?" he asks.

"Do you live near here?"

Michael frowns. "No. My grandparents do."

"You're not supposed to be in here, you know."

"Neither are *you!*" Michael spits. He feels a strange and sudden rage overcoming him. Somehow his childish anxiety over seeing an interloper in his sanctuary pales beneath a fiery anger, something near to hatred. It erupts with such sharpness that Michael actually feels himself flinch, as though he's been shocked by some hidden power line. Why should the girl anger him so? He wonders what it is about the nature of her innocuous questions that makes him despise her.

He pedals closer and is opening his mouth to say something, just what Michael isn't sure, when a searing glint on the girl's body forces him to screw up his face. Shielding his eyes with one hand, Michael gives the girl a long and scrutinizing glare.

And then he truly sees her...

Sees the flour-pale and bruise-blue pallor of her skin, sees the nuggets of crystallized water that form in her hair, in the folds of her oversized T-shirt, on her rigid ill-coloured limbs. Her eyes are almost solid white, but instinctively Michael knows that blindness is not the cause.

When she again asks Michael what his name is, her voice rises from somewhere in the gravel pits and not from her rigid face, for the girl's jaw remains locked. For a beat Michael wonders if she is frozen solid.

To answer this thought, the girl suddenly raises her ice-scabbed arms as if to claim him.

Michael's actions are so frantic they must appear as one vast and hectic gesture: the shriek, the rearing around of his bike, the aching, desperate scaling of the gravel

31

mound, the piercing push through the tear in the fence, the breathless race across the fields.

Michael rides. And rides.

The distance Michael places between himself and the gravel yard brings little relief. Not even the sight of his grandparents' home calms him. He rushes up their driveway, allows his bike to drop, then runs directly to the tiny guestroom that serves as his bedroom every summer vacation.

Burying his face in his pillow, Michael listens to the sound of approaching footsteps.

"Mikey, you all right?"

His grandmother's musical voice is a balm to him. Michael lifts his head, but when he sees the reddish stains that mar his grandmother's fingers and the apron she's wearing he winces.

"What is it, son?"

He points a bent finger and his grandmother laughs.

"It's strawberries, silly. I'm making jam. I saw you come tearing up the road like the devil himself was at your heels."

Michael wipes his mouth. "Grandma, do you believe in ghosts?"

Her brow lifts behind her spectacles. "Ghosts? No, I can't say that I do, Mikey. Why?"

His account of the experience reaches all the way to the tip of Michael's tongue, but at the last instant he bites it back. He shakes his head, stays silent.

His grandmother frowns. "Too much time in the sun, dear. Why don't you lie down for a while? I'll wake you for lunch."

Michael nods. His grandmother's suggestion sounds very good indeed. He reclines his head back onto the pillows and shuts out the world.

He doesn't realize he's dozed off until he feels his grandmother nudging him. Perspiration has dried on his hair and skin, which makes him feel clammy. He shivers and then groggily makes his way to the kitchen to join his grandparents for sandwiches.

"What happened, sleepyhead?" his grandfather teases. "You didn't tire yourself out on the first day, did you?"

His grandfather receives a sardonic swat from his grandmother, which makes Michael laugh.

"He probably just rode too long in the heat," she says.

"Oh? Where'd you ride to?"

"Just...around." Michael bites into his sandwich, hoping that this line of questioning will end.

"Mikey asked me a little earlier if I believed in ghosts." His grandmother sets a tumbler of milk down in front of Michael as she settles into her chair.

"Ghosts? What brought that on?"

Michael shrugs. "Nothing. I was just wondering."

He cannot be sure, but Michael feels that his grandfather's glare on him has hardened.

≈≈

Michael remains indoors, the only place he feels relatively secure, for the rest of the day. He helps his grandmother jar up the last of her jams and wash up afterwards. He watches cartoons while she prepares supper. His grandfather is outdoors, labouring on one of the seemingly endless projects which occupies so much of his time. He is a veritable stranger in the house. Last summer Michael had tried to assist him with the various chores, but he got the feeling that his grandfather found him more of a burden than an aid. So this year he takes his mother's advice and just stays out of his grandfather's way.

Though he's never been mean, his grandfather does give off an air that Michael finds far less pleasant than that of his grandmother. She is always cheerful, brimming with old family stories or ideas of various things that he could help her with. Grandma's chores never feel like work.

After supper Michael's mother phones to see how his first day went. He is oddly grateful for the deep homesickness that hearing her voice summons; it means that he doesn't have to think about what he'd seen that morning. His mother says she'll be up to visit on the weekend.

The late morning nap and mounting anxieties make sleep almost impossible for Michael. He lies in his bed, which suddenly feels uncomfortably foreign, and wrestles with the implications of what he has seen, what he has *experienced*, for the encounter was far more than visual. Standing in the presence of that girl, whatever she had been, made the world feel different. Just recollecting the event made Michael feel dizzy.

Maybe his grandmother is right, maybe he has been riding too hard under the hot sun. After a time Michael understands that the only way he can put the incident behind is to return to the pits, to test what he'd seen or thought he had seen. His teacher last year told him the first rule when learning about science and nature is that you must repeat the experiment. If you want to know the truth about something you have to do the same thing more than once. If the results are the same, then what you've found is something real.

Tomorrow he will go back. He will find the truth.

≈≈

The girl is nowhere to be found. Michael rides out after breakfast, despite his grandmother advising him against it. He promises her he will ride slowly and in the shade, and that he'll be home to help her with lunch.

Michael is so elated by the absence of the ugly vision that he plunges through the rip in the chain-link and begins to scale and shoot down the gravel mounds at a manic pace. Dust mushrooms up in his wake. Michael feels unfettered from everything.

The sound of an approaching vehicle startles him to such a degree that he almost loses his balance.

Glancing up to where the country lane meets the gate of the gravel pit, Michael spies his grandfather's pickup truck. He performs a quick shoulder check, panicked by the distance that stretches between him and the hole in the fence.

His grandfather steps out of the cab. Realizing that he has no time to escape, Michael hunches low and pedals behind the farthest gravel mound. There he dismounts, crouches, and is punished by the thundering heartbeat in his ears.

The gate is unlocked, de-chained. The pickup truck

comes crawling down along the narrow path, parking before the shed. Michael doesn't hear the engine shut off and he wonders if his grandfather is just waiting for him to come out from behind the mound so he can run him down.

But then the engine is silent and is soon followed by the rumbling sound which signifies the corrugated metal door being opened. Has the ghost-girl flung the door open from the inside? Perhaps she has attacked his grandfather. Michael swallows. With utmost caution he creeps to the edge of the mound and peers.

It is dark inside the shed, so dark that it looks boundless; a deep cavern of redbrick. Michael can just discern the faintest suggestions of objects: power tools, equipment of various shapes, overfilled shelves of metal. The only item that stands out is the white box. It glows against the gloom and puts Michael in mind of Dracula's coffin. But the sight of its orange power light glowing like a match flame confirms to Michael that it is nothing more than a freezer.

The shed's corrugated door is drawn down. His grandfather must have chores to attend to in the shed. It likely won't take him long to locate whatever tools he needs. Michael steals the opportunity to rush back to the tear and escape.

He races out to the bridge above West Creek. There he settles into a shady spot, dangles his legs over the bridge's edge and studies catfish squirming along the current. Near noon, Michael mounts his bike and rides back to his grandparents' home.

The pickup truck is parked in the driveway. He takes a deep breath, praying that his grandfather hasn't seen him making his escape.

"I'm home, grandma," he calls from the foyer.

Entering the kitchen, Michael is startled by the sight of his grandfather fidgeting at the counter.

"She went into town to run some errands," he says. "Sit down, your lunch is ready."

Michael does as he is told. His grandfather plunks down a bowl of stewed tomatoes before him, along with a glass of milk. He nests himself at the far end of the table and chews in silence.

His stomach knots. Michael chokes down the slippery fruit in his bowl.

"I suppose I should have had you wash your hands before we sat down," his grandfather remarks. "You're pretty filthy. You've got dust all over your clothes and hands."

Michael freezes. His grandfather's gaze remains fixed on the food in his dish, which he spoons up and eats in a measured rhythm.

When his bowl is empty, his grandfather sets down his spoon and lifts his eyes to Michael's. "I have a confession to make," he begins. "You know yesterday when your grandmother brought up the topic of ghosts? Well, can you keep a secret, just between us?"

Michael nods.

"You swear it?"

"I swear."

"Cross your heart?"

Michael does so.

"All right then. I wasn't being honest when I said I didn't believe in them. The fact is I do. I saw a ghost once myself."

"You did?"

"Yes. Well, it was something *like* a ghost. I think what I saw was actually a jinn."

"A jinn?"

"A jinn is a spirit, Michael. Legend says they are created by fire. They can take all kinds of forms; animals, people. But they're very dangerous."

"What did the jinn that you saw look like?" Michael asks breathlessly.

"It was in the form of a young girl."

Michael feels his palms growing damp. "Where did you see her?"

"In the woods, not too far from here. I think she was planning to burn the forest down. That's what the jinn do; they bring fire."

"And did she?"

His grandfather shakes his head.

"So what happened?"

His grandfather tents his hands before him. "They say the only way to combat the element of fire is with ice..."

And with that, a silent tension coils between child and elder, winding tighter like a spring. Michael is confused, curious, and scared. He doesn't know what to do or say.

"Young boys get curious, and when they get curious they sometimes discover things that give them the wrong impression of what the world is like. There are always two sides to things, Michael," his grandfather advises. "There is the appearance of things and then there is what lies beneath. I want you to remember that, boy. Don't base your opinions of the world on how it appears. Always try to remember what lies beneath. Sometimes the things that appear to be the most innocent are the most dangerous, and vice versa. It was a long time before I knew this, so I want you to learn it while you're young. You understand?"

Michael nods even though he does not at all understand.

The sound of his grandmother turning into the driveway brings Michael a relief that borders on gleeful. He runs to her. His grandfather rises and dutifully clears the table.

≈≈

The remainder of the day moves at a crawl as Michael searches for a way to probe his grandfather further about the jinn. Is this what he has seen? No, what he's seen looks more like a spirit born of ice. Either way, the woods that surrounded the old gravel pits are obviously haunted, and that means they are dangerous. By bedtime that night Michael has resolved to never again visit the gravel pits. He will find other ways to amuse himself.

He has almost managed to convince himself that everything is right with the world when the girl appears again, this time inside his grandparents' house.

It is the dead of night and Michael is returning to his bed after relieving himself. She stands in the hallway, her flesh phosphorescent in the darkness. The nuggets of ice sparkle in her hair like a constellation of fallen stars.

Michael is bolted in place. His jaw falls open as if weighted. He looks at her but somehow isn't truly seeing her. In the back of his mind Michael wonders if what he is experiencing is what lies beneath the surface of the girl and not merely her appearance.

The girl neither speaks nor moves. She stands like a coldly morbid statue, with one arm jutting toward the wall of the corridor.

Michael's gaze hesitantly runs along the length of the girl's extended arm, and her pointing finger. Is she indicating the unused phone jack on the wall? Michael turns back to face her but before him there now stretches only darkness.

He lingers in the vacated hallway for eons before finally crouching down to investigate the phone jack. It is set into the moulding, which Michael's grandmother always keeps clean and waxed. Michael clasps the jack's white plastic covering and tugs at it. It pops loose.

Within it Michael discovers a pair of keys. One of them is larger than the other and has the words 'Tuff Lock' engraved on its head. The smaller key is unmarked.

A creak of wood somewhere inside the house acts as a warning to Michael. He hurriedly recovers the jack and slips back to his room where he lies in thought until the sun at last burns away the shadows.

≈≈

Only after he hears his grandfather fire up his old pickup and drive off—Is he going back to his secret redbrick vault at the gravel pits?—does Michael leave his room.

His grandmother is sitting on the living room sofa. She seems smaller somehow, almost deflated.

"Morning," Michael says, testing her mood.

"Good morning, dear," she replies. Her tone is distant, a swirl of unfocused words.

"Where's grandpa?"

She stands. "He had some chores to do. Are you hungry?" She advances to the kitchen without waiting for Michael's response.

"You all right, grandma?"

She forces a chortle. "I'm fine, Mikey, just fine. Your grandpa just seemed a little out of sorts this morning and I guess I'm a bit worried about him, that's all."

Michael feels his face flush. "What's the matter with

him?"

"He didn't sleep well." She seems to be attempting to drown out her own voice by clattering pans and beating eggs in a chrome bowl. "Your grandpa has bad dreams sometimes, and when he does he wakes up very cranky and fidgety."

"Oh."

When they sit down to eat Michael wrestles to find what he hopes is a clever method of interrogation. He needs so badly to know...

"Does grandpa ever talk about what his bad dreams are about?"

"No."

"Do you ever have bad dreams?"

"Almost never, dear. I think the last time was a couple years ago when there was some bad business here in the village."

"What happened?"

"A girl went missing." She speaks the words more into her coffee cup than to Michael, but even muffled they stun him.

"Missing?"

His grandmother nods. "She was one of the summer people, came up here with her family. I'd see her walking to and from the beach almost every day by herself. Then one day she went down to swim but never came back. Must have drowned, poor thing. They dragged the lake but she was never found. A terrible event. Felt so bad for her mother and father. That's why your grandfather and I never let you go the beach unsupervised."

"Do you remember what she looked like?"

She shrugs. "Thirteen-years-old or so. Blonde hair, I recall that much."

Michael excuses himself from the table. His jimmying open of the phone jack is masked by the noises of his grandmother washing the breakfast dishes.

"Think I'll go for a ride," he tells her.

"Be careful, dear. Have fun."

≈≈

Throughout his race to the gravel pits Michael senses that

39

the village is somehow made out of eyes. He passes no one, but is terrified by the prospect of encountering his grandfather at the pits.

The area is equally abandoned. The cavern of redbrick sits snugly locked, illuminated by a hot dappling of sunlight. He enters the breach in the fence and fishes out the pair of keys from his pocket.

He marries the one labelled Tuff Lock with the padlock that bears the same engraving. The lock gives easily. The clunking noise startles a murder of crows from their nest. Michael cries out at their sudden cawing, wing-flapping reprimand. He quickly looks about, terrified of being caught.

The gravel mounds are as ancient hills, silent and patient and indifferent to all human activity. Michael removes the padlock and struggles to raise the corrugated door. It rattles up its track, revealing the musty, cluttered darkness.

Like an ember, the orange light of the freezer gleams from the back of the shed.

Michael feels about for a light switch but finds none. With great care he makes his way to the light. He is like a solider crossing a minefield. Every motorized tool, every stack of bagged soil, is a danger.

He reaches the freezer. Its surface is gritty with dust. He sees the metal clamp that holds its lid shut. It is secured with another padlock. Before he's fully realized what he is doing, Michael inserts the smaller key and frees the open padlock from its loop. He can hear the freezer buzzing and he wonders if he is truly ready to see what it contains.

'You've gone this far,' he tells himself. He pulls the lid up from the frame.

Frost funnels upward, riding on the gust of manufactured arctic air. Like ghosts, the cold smoke flies and vanishes.

A bundled canvas tarp reposes within the freezer's bunk. Its folds are peppered with ice, its drab earthy brownness in sharp contrast to the white banks of frost that have accumulated on the old freezer's walls. The tarp is secured with butcher's twine, which Michael cannot break, so instead he wriggles one of the canvas flaps until his aching fingers can do no more.

But what he has done is enough. Through the small part in the bundle the whitish, lidless eye stares back at him, like a waxing moon orbiting in the microcosmic blackness of the canvas shroud.

Michael whimpers. All manner of emotion assails him at once, rendering him wordless.

A shadow steps in front of the open shed door. Michael spins around, allowing the freezer lid to slam down. His grandfather has caught him. Michael sees his future as one encased in stifling ice.

But the figure in the doorway is too slight to be his grandfather.

Michael then sees the ghost-eyes staring at him from the dim face. A face that is brightened by rows of teeth as the girl grins. She bolts off into the woods.

"Wait!" Michael cries. He stumbles across the littered shed, but by the time he reaches the gravel pits she has gone.

What do I do? Michael keeps thinking as he locks both freezer and shed. He needs help.

His confusion blurs the ride back to his grandmother.

It also makes him doubt what he sees once the house comes into view.

His grandfather's pickup is once more in the driveway. Beyond it the entire house is engulfed in flames.

Neighbours are rushing about the property, seemingly helpless. Michael speeds up to the lawn, jumps off his bike and attempts to run through the front door.

A man stops him. "No, son! We've called the fire department. Stay back, stay back!"

Ushered to the edge of his grandparents' property, Michael can see the window of their bedroom. The lace curtain is being eaten by fire, allowing him a heat-weepy view of the figures that are lying on the twin beds inside. He sees his grandmother, who appears to be bound to her bed with ropes. Next to her, Michael's grandfather lies unbound, a willing sacrifice. The large can of gasoline stands on the floor between them. The pane shatters from the heat.

Michael feels his gaze being tugged to the trees at the

end of the yard, where some kind of animal is skittering up the limbs with ease.

In the distance, sirens are wailing their lament.

LAUDATE DOMINUM
(for many voices)

D. P. Watt

'*How* things are in the world is a matter of complete indifference for
what is higher. God does not reveal himself *in* the world.'
Ludwig Wittgenstein, *Tractatus Logico-Philosophicus*

Sitting on a bench, on the outer harbour wall, wrapped
in a wintery coat—despite the encouraging sun of a
late March afternoon—we find Stephen Walker. He is
eating an egg mayonnaise sandwich and drinking from a
flask of tea, both prepared that morning in his holiday
cottage in the seaside village of Polperro. He has just
returned from today's walk, this time along the nine miles
of coastal path to Fowey, and back again. Holidaying, for
Stephen Walker, was less a relaxation than a
demonstration of vitality.

His demeanour might once have been termed—some
years ago now—curmudgeonly. Today he might, more
straightforwardly, be described as a 'grumpy old man',
now that such nomenclature is popular, and always
assigned with mocking affection. Of course the fault for
this miserable attitude lay not with him, but rather with
everyone else. As he was fond of telling anyone who
would listen, the problem with today's youth was the lack
of military service. Despite having served only three

months in the Ordnance corps, before being invalided out (a detail always omitted in the retelling), it had, apparently, been 'the making of him.' Young people today had no *stamina*, no *will*, and no *backbone*.

It was no surprise then to find him holidaying alone in Cornwall, a place that had been dear to him for many years, mostly for its seclusion (if you chose the right places) and beautiful coastal walks. He would visit most years in late March, to take advantage of the last few weeks before the place hummed with tourists and their children, dogs and ice creams.

Whenever visiting Polperro, and when the place was available, he liked to hire a small cottage at the end of The Warren that Oscar Kokoschka had spent time in during the war, painting the outer harbour repeatedly. As an amateur oil painter himself Stephen Walker liked to feel that a little genius might rub off on him by inhabiting the dwelling of one of his favourite artists.

Painting and walking; two wonderful pursuits, balancing the equal requirements of every human being: quiet, contemplative creativity and vigorous, outdoor exercise.

Whilst he was naturally frugal he was certainly not mean. He was, *how do they say it*, careful. His savings from lunch would then contribute towards that evening's treats; real ale, crab salad, and sticky toffee pudding and custard, at The Blue Peter. This was a small inn only a few feet away from him, and a place he always enjoyed spending a couple of evenings at during his holiday.

You can imagine him though, there at one of the larger window seats, begrudging sharing his table with a young family that have nowhere else to sit; the children staring up at the curious man uneasily, their dog occasionally nuzzling at his crotch.

To avoid unwanted small talk he takes a leaflet from one of those racks advertising local attractions and unfolds it across the table so that he should not be interrupted during his meal.

'The Looe Valley line.'

His eyes are drawn to a picture on the inside flap, of a small well, rather mossy and overgrown—'St Keyne wishing well,' read the caption, with an arrow pointing to one of the stops on the railway line. There were a couple of stanzas of poetry beneath that, by Robert Southey, the second mentioned that the well was surrounded by an oak, an ash, an elm and a willow tree. Apparently, the leaflet went on, 'Whichever of a married couple drinks first from the well, they will "wear the trousers." So, hurry, lest your spouse beats you to it!' Despite this folklore nonsense it sounded intriguing. Also, the leaflet proclaimed, 'On your way back from the well why not visit The Mechanical Music Museum, where you will find all manner of music playing devices from yesteryear!'

It was rare that Stephen Walker was interested in anything of the kind, believing that most of them were aimed at extorting money from gullible parents through the relentless, imploring nagging of their children. Such as those sat opposite him now, slurping their cheap cola through bendy straws, and squabbling over their crisps. But, he was certain, there would be few children desperate to go to this museum; they were not interested in the magic of yesteryear's innovations, the spirit of the craftsman and the skill of the mechanic.

He would visit the museum the very next morning, he resolved. He drained the rest of his beer and headed back to the cottage, planning his day.

First, a brisk walk along the coastal path to Looe—he would have completed the five miles of it before most of the nation's adolescents were awake, he chuckled. And he would then be on the train to visit the St Keyne wishing well, then take in the museum on his way back, before continuing to Liskeard to round the day off.

≈≈

The walk went to plan, although the steep paths and cliffs to Looe, especially around Talland Bay, seemed to take their toll on him more this time than when he had last walked them a few years previously. He had over an hour to kill before the train at 10:32. He browsed around some shops, but didn't buy anything.

The train was on time, and he enjoyed the restful juddering of the carriage as it made its gentle way through some splendid scenery. The ticket inspector had informed him that St Keyne was a 'request' stop and he would let the driver know. If only all train services these days had such courteous and helpful staff, Stephen Walker mused.

He alighted on a deserted platform, with newly painted white picket fencing, with a quaint passenger shelter. He could almost be back in the 1950s he thought, even though for the most part, he already was.

He checked his watch. 10:50. He had over two hours before the next train at 12:59 that would take him on for the afternoon to Liskeard. This should be plenty of time to find the well and then return to explore the museum.

He headed off up the steep lane into the village of St Keyne, eager to find this beautiful little wishing well. Who knows, he thought, even this late in life I might find a wife, and if so I'll have one up on her by having drunk at it first. He laughed quietly, at the improbability of either event.

The well proved elusive though. The little map on his leaflet did not appear to scale and he found himself trekking across some muddy fields, looking this way and that, without any idea of where he was. He headed back to the main road and back down the steep, narrow lane, towards the railway station.

Then he spotted—just where the steep lane joined the larger road at the top of the village—a signpost, mostly covered by low hanging branches. In his eagerness to rush on he must have missed it.

It did not prove particularly informative though. One side pointed north, saying 'St Keyne Wishing Well,' and the other, pointing south, read exactly the same. Some local was clearly having a joke on the tourists. Stephen Walker did not really consider himself a tourist and was not amused.

He consulted his watch. 12:30. That damned wishing well really had taken some time up. He needed to get to the museum before the train arrived at 12:59.

Then the thought struck him, he could catch a later one. Why waste the opportunity to enjoy the musical machines when he could catch the *next* train to Liskeard. He filled a pipe—a little luxury he allowed himself only when out walking—and consulted the timetable again. It would have to be the 14:30. Oh well, why not take things easy, and with a little shrug of the shoulders he ambled down the lane to visit the museum.

Had he looked a little further behind the signpost he would have seen a set of greenish crumbling steps leading down to the wishing well. There were no longer any trees beside it, if ever there had been. And whether it was a magical well or not would have to remain a mystery. All that was forgotten now; Stephen Walker had set a new itinerary.

As he took slow puffs on the pipe he found himself humming a little tune, as the museum came into view. This was most unusual as he did not approve of humming. Still, it didn't hurt did it, out here where there was nobody to hear him. It showed that he was taking full advantage of his leisure time.

The sign for the 'Mechanical Music Museum' pointed to a large industrial building with corrugated roof that lay behind a cottage. Some steep steps led down to them both and Stephen surmised the owner of the museum must also live in the cottage. As he tapped his pipe out on the wall at the top of the steps he heard a wonderful chorus of song coming from the museum. It sounded like a choir rehearsing. He listened a while. He was not sure what the hymn was, but it was delightful, and he spent a minute or two enjoying it.

The choir finished the hymn as he got to the bottom of the steps. Stephen was relieved as he hadn't wanted to interrupt their practice; perhaps they shared the building with the museum.

He poked his head through the door, even though the sign read 'closed.' The building might even have been a warehouse once, so vast was the space inside. At the far end there were great red curtains that gave the place the feel of a village hall, sometimes used for local am-dram performances no doubt. All about the perimeter of the building were varying musical devices, maybe a dozen or so, ranging in size from small gramophones to larger organs.

There was a tall man, maybe in his early sixties, standing some distance away. He was dressed in scruffy work clothes and seemed quite busy. But there was certainly no choir. It must have been a recording, Stephen thought, even though it had been quite loud.

The tall man spotted him and shook his head apologetically.

"Oh, I'm sorry, sir," the man said, depositing a handful of wooden blocks onto a workbench. "We don't open to visitors until April. It takes so much to maintain all of these machines that I have to use all of the winter months to keep them in pristine condition."

"Ah, I see . . ." Stephen began.

"I'm working flat out on these dampers as it is," he interrupted, gesturing to the blocks and a scattering of felt and leather patches strewn across the bench.

"Oh dear," Stephen said, "how disappointing. I had hoped so much to see the place before I leave for home in a few days. I recall my grandfather had a music machine in the living room; it played great metal disks, and even had a clock in it too."

"An old upright, eh!" the man said, his eyes bright and his face suddenly interested, as though a little switch had been flicked somewhere inside him. "It will have been a Polyphon, no doubt, or maybe even a rare Symphonion."

"That was *it!*" Stephen said, the name suddenly bringing back his grandfather's pronunciation of it. "Sym*phon*-ion! He'd always say, after we'd had some lunch, 'Shall we have a few tunes from *Mr Sym*phon*ion*.' And my sister and I would be delighted. The *Symphionion*—well I never . . ."

"Might I ask, sir, do you sing?" the man said, rather incongruously.

Stephen Walker was perplexed. "Do I sing?"

"Yes," the man said, as though his sudden change of topic were entirely appropriate. "Do you belong to a choir? Do you *sing*?"

"Er, no, well, I mean, not for many years now, not since I was a child," Stephen replied, feeling rather badgered by a certain school-masterly tone the man had adopted.

"I was particularly struck by the quality of your voice, you see," the man continued, heading over to him. "It has depth, and richness. But is that tobacco I smell? It would be a shame to spoil such a wonderful voice with the *evil weed* now wouldn't it."

"I've just had a pipe, as a matter of fact, on my way down from the wishing well—a wishing well that I couldn't damned well find," Stephen said, defensively. "But I don't really see what business my smoking habits are . . ."

"No doubt the Connor boys have been playing with the well signposts again," the man interrupted, offering his hand in greeting. "I'm Philip Morin, owner, restorer and guide here at the Mechanical Music Museum."

"I'm Mr Walker, Stephen Walker," he replied, shaking Philip's hand timidly, without having shaken the sense of being rather admonished.

"Let me show you around then, Mr Walker," Philip said (the issue of being closed for the season apparently having been entirely forgotten).

"My own grandfather was an actor, I come from a long line of performers," he said, going over to a small, dark wooden box. "This is one of the earliest machines I have, and one of great sentimental value." Philip seemed a connoisseur of the non-sequitur.

He cranked a handle a few times and opened the lid. What looked like a black wax cylinder was spinning inside. From underneath the table he produced a large metal horn, fluted and almost shell-like. He attached the horn to a pivot arm and rested the base of it, housing a large needle, on the thick cylinder.

An eerie noise came out, mostly a great cloud of static and white noise, but in the background one could just make out a voice, but not the words.

"This is my grandfather," he said, proudly, "reading Dickens' *Christmas Carol* in 1896."

Stephen was still unable to make out the words. All he could discern was a strange echoing of the sentences going on within the machine.

"It takes a while to warm up," Philip said, "like any voice really."

He angled a lamp down close to the cylinder, to warm it. "Perhaps we can try that one again later when the old man's back in tune."

Then, the sound seemed to clarify and there was a

49

great laugh from the reader, Philip's grandfather, followed by a peal of bells—Scrooge on Christmas morning, without a doubt!

"Marvellous," Stephen exclaimed.

"Yes, it is rather, isn't it," Philip said. "This voice, my ancestor's, brought to life here for us, one hundred years later. For all of its terrible crimes there are also some miraculous things achieved through technology."

"Yes, it really must have been magical to hear the human voice reproduced through a machine in that fashion, for the first time," Stephen said.

"Indeed," Philip replied. "But what of the instruments that *played themselves*, they would have been no less incredible."

He led Stephen over to a fairly ordinary looking upright black piano. In the centre of it, where the music stand would have been, there were two horizontal bars, onto which Philip locked a long roll of thick punched paper. It looked a bit like the paper cards he had used many years before in the computer room at the post office, where he had worked briefly as an apprentice.

Having threaded the roll Philip then set about dismantling the front of the machine so that they could get a good look at the mechanism.

"Now this one was made by an incredible craftsman," Philip began. "Ernst Steget of Berlin. He engineered the pianos, but he couldn't produce the musical rolls. This had to be done by another craftsman, Giovanni Galuppo, down the road from him. However, Steget was fond of a schnapps, or two, in the local bar of an evening."

They both laughed, in the conspiratorial fashion that late middle-aged men do when issues of alcohol surface—such false bonhomie; beneath the forced laughter only half-remembered conquests that were never really conquered, opportunities squandered by a loose tongue, loved ones slighted and friends abused.

"Sadly, his love of the schnapps resulted in the gradual dwindling of his business and eventually he became so indebted to Galuppo that he had to go and work for him to pay it all off," Philip continued. "Such is the way of the world I'm afraid, when one's bounty and talents are squandered on *vice*."

Stephen didn't like the tone of that last remark, aimed—as it clearly was—at his own indulgence in a pipe or two. But he did not have time to dwell upon the slight, if such it was, as the piano suddenly erupted into sound and motion. The keys danced beneath invisible fingers and the inside of the machine was feverish with the work of pulleys and wheels, valves, bellows and levers, all animated by the little blank squares on the paper roll as it slid through the instrument like a great white tongue.

"What use the pianist, eh?" Stephen joked.

"Oh, we still have our uses, Mr Walker, with the right instrument," Philip retorted, rather viciously, Stephen felt.

Then a shrill electronic ring called out from the workbench, crashing the world back into the present. Philip went over to answer a cordless telephone and then called out. "It's my wife, there's a delivery for me. I'll be back in a moment. I'll bring some tea too, enjoy the rest of the tune!"

Stephen smiled and nodded. The piano was playing away and he felt rather nostalgic for the music his parents would entertain him with on the record player when he was a boy. His father loved the old music hall ones, and the spoken word records. The hours they would spend together on a Sunday listening to Flanders and Swann, or old Henry Hall and the BBC orchestra on scratchy 78s.

The paper was still rolling around as Philip returned with a tray laden with cups, saucers, milk jug and a great steaming pot of tea. There was also a plate of biscuits, enough to service an AGM of the Women's Institute, Stephen thought.

"Doris thought you might be a bit peckish, so she put out some biscuits," Philip said, carefully balancing the crammed tray on a little stool beside a low chair with rather grubby paisley upholstery. "It's Earl Grey, I hope that's ok."

Stephen smiled and nodded.

"I thought you were an Earl Grey chap," Philip said. "I didn't know if you took it with milk or lemon, so there's both."

"Oh, milk for me please," Stephen said, his knees bending a little to the tune still tinkling from the piano.

"I thought so, milk it is, do help yourself," Philip said. "I hope you don't mind, I must help this driver with some items I've had shipped over. I shan't be a moment. You carry on, there's a good few minutes left on that reel, I'm sure you won't be bored."

"Oh, most certainly not," Stephen replied. For the first time in many years—despite Philip's frosty undercurrents—he felt he had discovered a kindred spirit.

He must have listened to the piano for too long, carried back to hedonistic Weimar, for when he poured himself a cup of tea it tasted a little odd, rather sour. Stewed probably. That, or the milk was off. He gave the little jug a sniff. Yes, it was the milk. Never mind, he needed a little refreshment now, as it might be some time before he got to Liskeard and found a tearoom. What was it mother used to say—a few germs won't kill you! He poured himself another cup and as the last few notes on the piano tinkled out, and the scroll of paper unravelled its last coded dots, he looked about the expansive building.

As he had noted on his arrival the place was by no means full of instruments. Each had its own particular space. Some were small, like the little wax cylinder player he had heard Philip's grandfather reading Dickens upon; some larger, such as the piano from Berlin in the 20s. There were some larger organs on the other side of the room, one near the large curtain across the back wall. This seemed much like the kind of grand Wurlitzer organs he'd seen as a child, both in the theatre and at the fairs. It would be wonderful to hear Philip play that when he returned. Behind that though, and rather oddly positioned, was something more individual. It looked like quite a small organ, and Stephen thought it may have been uniquely crafted, so unusual was its construction. There seemed to be no ornate element to it, all was pure function. The panelling had obviously been crafted from a variety of different woods, each giving their particular rich colour to the overall piecemeal effect. And, from where he was standing, he could see no discernible maker's plate.

Finishing his second tea in a swift gulp, Stephen walked over and inspected it cautiously. As he had first thought, there seemed to be no maker's mark (emblazoned proudly upon all the other machines) and none of the keys, or mechanical dials and knobs had any lettering, or numbers upon them, as was common on the other models. Perhaps this was in the first stages of restoration he thought, running a hand along its well polished, although awkwardly constructed, wooden frame.

He thought he heard a noise then, from within it; a sort of escape of air. Perhaps a valve or piston decompressing.

It quite startled him, and he jumped a little.

Shh. Shh. It came again, twice, but sounded so like someone shushing a crowd to be quiet before a performance began that he didn't know what to make of it.

He looked around to check that Philip hadn't come back yet from unloading the delivery van. He didn't want to look a fool, and didn't want to be noticed touching something that was probably delicate and very expensive.

But, he just couldn't help himself.

He pressed one of the keys.

From the back of the instrument there came a voice— *lah!*

There could be no mistaking it; this was the sound of a *human voice*, singing a note. Stephen was intrigued, and a little disturbed. This latter sentiment did not prevent him from trying again though. He pressed the same key, and another one from nearer the other end of the board. A soprano voice sang out, at the same time as an alto joined in. But they did not sound recorded, it seemed as though the singers stood right beside him.

He shivered a little, but determined that it must be due to the cold of the airy industrial building. It was not particularly cold that day, and besides Philip had turned the storage heaters on only the week before and they were pumping dry, warm air around the building to fend off any chill.

Despite his fear, Stephen shuffled cautiously around the back of the machine to find where the 'voices' were coming from. There was a wooden grill at the back, rather like an old speaker. A faint draught was coming from it, and upon that delicate air there wafted an odd, meaty scent, as of cured European sausages.

He noticed that above the speaker there was a panel of some sort, made of long timbers of what could only be olive wood; their swirling grains and strange knots had been lovingly jointed together and finished with a little latch of leather and a bone toggle. This gave a strangely archaic feel to the instrument. Yet, all of this did not dissuade Stephen Walker from loosening the cord and carefully easing the panel down.

At first he thought they were the chicks of large birds, all arrayed on wooden plinths, calling, silently, for food. So bizarre was the thing before him that it took a moment for his mind to fully comprehend what he was witnessing.

These were the organ pipes, and each an *organ,* of sorts.

There were about twenty large wooden tubes, rather like inverted didgeridoos, in three rows of varying height. Each was crafted from a different wood and atop many of them there was stretched a thin, pulsating blob of organic tissue, with an oval opening across the top of the tube. There were five blank pipes.

Each fleshy aperture slowly opened and closed, like a gaping raw mouth, and dripped a clear fluid down the pipe which collected in metal trays below, in which there rested a number of short sticks, each wrapped with swabs of cloth soaked in this thick liquid.

The smell was foul, but in the face of such horror that was the least arresting detail.

Stephen Walker was appalled. Yet he could not shake off a perverse desire to touch one of these things; to run his finger across it—there was something sadly familiar about their monstrosity. Almost against his will his hand reached slowly forward.

Then a voice echoed across the cavernous space.

It was Philip, returned from his delivery.

"How you getting on in here?" he called, merrily, wiping his oily hands with a rag.

As surreptitiously as he could, and with a terror welling within him, Stephen Walker slid the wooden panel back into place and carefully fastened the toggle, as

Philip approached him, smiling his cheery smile.

"I was just, erm, admiring the woodwork on this one," Stephen said, shakily. He felt rather dizzy all of a sudden, hot and flustered. "It's very . . . beautiful . . ."

"Oh, that's a little pet project of mine," Philip said, making his way over to the larger Wurlitzer organ. "I'm afraid it isn't in full working order at the moment so I can't play you a tune on it yet; maybe one day, when I get the time to finish it."

Stephen felt sick, claustrophobic and terrified. He was nervous that if he even made an attempt to move he would faint.

"This little beauty is my pride and joy," Philip began, seating himself at the controls of the vast organ; controls that looked more like a spacecraft than a musical instrument.

Philip flicked a switch and the huge red curtains at the back of the building rolled back to reveal an array of shiny metal pipes, row upon row of them.

Stephen Walker could think of nothing but the fleshy, gaping wounds calling out silently in the contraption behind him.

"Now, Mr Walker," Philip shouted out. "Give it your best voice. I'll keep it simple, don't you worry."

A great flare of sound assailed Stephen from the rows of pipes.

Roll out the barrel! What a ridiculous song to hear only moments after having made his horrifying discovery. Stephen just managed to stop himself vomiting.

"Come on," shouted Philip, his upper body rocking about like some demented toy. "Join in! *We'll have a barrel of fun* . . ."

Stephen mumbled a few words in an attempt to show willing, "*We've got the blues on the run.*"

"Oh, *Mr Walker*, give it some *oomph!*" Philip cried, clearly getting irritated.

Stephen Walker gave in. His head was spinning and the whole place began to look blurry and distorted. He tried to turn the insanity of the situation to his advantage—to get a bit of courage up.

"*Ring out a song of good cheer,*" Stephen belted out. Quite where the spirit came from to sing in such an absurd situation he didn't know. *"Now's the time to roll the barrel, for the gang's all here . . ."*

"Now *that's* what I'm talking about, *Stephen*," Philip said, ceasing his playing.

It was the first time he had addressed Stephen Walker by his Christian name and something in the intonation was sinister and threatening. "What a beautiful baritone you have there, *Stephen*; real quality, and something we're sorely lacking here in our little choir."

It may have been the blast of noise, or his own singing, or even Philip's ominous tone, that had disoriented him, but Stephen Walker felt most peculiar.

He staggered a little and slumped in the paisley chair to get his strength back, strength he would need if he were to get away from this crazy man. The seat was weak though and the bottom gave way. He crumpled into it like a rag doll, arms and legs at ridiculous angles. He hadn't the energy left to correct his posture; his arms felt numb, his legs useless. His eyelids were heavy, and his mouth dry. He just sat there as everything around him became hazier, and darker, imploring Philip to help him with lips that merely twitched rather than pronouncing words.

Philip sat down opposite him, getting blurrier by the moment. He poured himself a cup of Earl Grey, dropping a slice of lemon into it with a sad chuckle.

"I always take it with lemon, and *plenty* of sugar," he said, sniffing at the milk jug, "besides the milk is always a bit funny at this time of year, I find."

Stephen made one last effort to get up. He succeeded only in knocking the chair into the little stool sending the tray crashing to the concrete floor.

The teapot, jug, cup and saucer all shattered.

"Oh, never mind," Philip said, "Doris has plenty of spares. It's worth it anyway; you don't know how hard it is to get people to join the choir out here. Trust me, I'll be able to take much better care of that voice than you have.

"I hope you understand, *Stephen*.

"What is it the good book says, *I will sing with the spirit, and I will sing with the understanding also.* It is best this way; your gifts will be most *cherished*—dutifully *maintained."*

Stephen couldn't speak.
He couldn't move.

≈≈

As the lights dimmed in Stephen Walker's eyes Philip
Morin took up his seat at the other, primitive, grotesque
organ, looking every bit the maestro. And as he played
the building filled with strange, lonely voices; exultant in
mechanical agony, rapturous in automatic praise. Their
beautiful, tortured song carried across the fields to fall
upon the ears of the grazing cattle and sheep, and was
drowned only momentarily by the 15:41 from Liskeard to
Looe, filled with schoolchildren returning home, eager to
forget their last class of the day. It did not stop at St
Keyne, for nobody was waiting on the platform, and few
ever alighted there.

MOONSTRUCK

Karin Tidbeck

They lived on the top floor in a building on the city's outskirts. If the stars were out, visitors would come, usually an adult with a child in tow. Alia would open the door and drop a curtsy to the visitors, who bade her good evening and asked for Doctor Kazakoff. Alia would run halfway up the stairs to the attic and call for the Doctor. At the same time, Father would emerge from the kitchen in a gentle blast of tea-scented air. Sometimes he had his apron on, and brought a whiff of baking bread. He would extend a knobby hand to pat the child's head, and then shake hands with the adult, whom he'd invite into the kitchen. While the parent (or grandparent, or guardian) hung their coat on a peg and sat down by the kitchen table, Father poured tea and wound up the gramophone. Then Mother, Doctor Kazakoff, would arrive, descending the spiral staircase in her blue frock and dark hair in a messy bun. She'd smile vaguely at the visiting child without making eye contact, and wave him or her over. They'd ascend the stairs to the darkened attic and out onto the little balcony, where the telescope stood. A stool sat below it, at just the right height for a child to climb up and look into the eyepiece.

Alia would crawl into an armchair in the shadows of the attic and watch the silhouettes of Mother and the visiting child, outlined against the faint starlight. Mother aimed the telescope toward some planet or constellation she found interesting, and stood aside so that the child could look. If it was a planet, Mother would rattle off facts. Alia preferred when she talked about constellations. She would pronounce each star's name slowly, as if tasting them: *Betelgeuse. Rigel. Bellatrix. Mintaka. Alnilam. Alnitak.* Alia saw them in her mind's eye, burning spheres rolling through the darkness with an inaudible thunder that resonated in her chest.

After a while, Mother would abruptly shoo the child away and take his or her place at the telescope. It was Alia's task to take the child by the hand and explain that Doctor Kazakoff meant no harm, but that telescope time was over now. Sometimes the child said goodbye to Mother's back. Sometimes they got a hum in reply. More often not. Mother was busy recalibrating the telescope.

When the moon was full, Mother wouldn't receive visitors. She would sit alone at the ocular and mumble to herself: the names of the seas, the highlands, the craters. Those nights (or days) she stayed up until the moon set.

≈≈

On the day it happened, Alia was twelve years old and home from school with a cold. That morning she found a brown stain in her underwear. It took a moment to realize what had really happened. She rifled through the cabinet under the sink for Mother's box of napkins, and found a pad that she awkwardly fastened to her panties. It rustled as she pulled them back up. She went back into the living room. The grandfather clock next to the display case showed a quarter past eleven.

"Today, at a quarter past eleven," she told the display case, "I became a woman."

Alia looked at her image in the glass. The person standing there, with pigtails and round cheeks and dressed in a pair of striped pyjamas, didn't look much like a woman. She sighed and crawled into the sofa with a blanket, rehearsing what to tell Mother when she came home.

≈≈

When the front door slammed a little later, Alia walked into the hallway. Mother stood there in a puff of cold air. She was home much too early.

"Mother," Alia began.

"Hello," said Mother. Her face was rigid, her eyes large and feverish. Without giving Alia so much as a glance, she took her coat off, dropped it on the floor and stalked up the attic stairs. Alia went after her out onto the balcony. Mother said nothing, merely stared upward. She wore a broad grin that looked misplaced in her stern face. Alia followed her gaze.

The moon hung in the zenith of the washed-out autumn sky, white and full in the afternoon light. It was much too large, and in the wrong place. Alia held out a hand at arm's length; the moon's edges circled her palm. She remained on the balcony, dumbfounded, until Father's thin voice called up to them from the hallway.

≈≈

Mother had once said that when Alia had her first period, they would celebrate and she would get to pick out her first ladies' dress. When Alia caught her attention long enough to tell her what happened, Mother just nodded. She showed Alia where the napkins were and told her to put stained clothes and sheets in cold water. Then she returned to the attic. Father walked around the flat, cleaning and fiddling in quick movements. He baked bread, loaf after loaf. Every now and then he came into the living room where Alia sat curled up in the sofa, and gave her a wordless hug.

≈≈

The radio blared all night. All the transmissions were about what had happened that morning at quarter past eleven. The president spoke to the nation: *We urge everyone to live their lives as usual. Go to work, go to school, but don't stay outside for longer than necessary. We don't yet know exactly what has happened, but our experts are*

61

investigating the issue. For your peace of mind, avoid looking up.

Out in the street, people were looking up. The balconies were full of people looking up. When Alia went to bed, Mother was still outside with her eye to the ocular. Father came to tuck Alia in. She pressed her face into his aproned chest, drawing in the smell of yeasty dough and after-shave.

"What if it's my fault?" she whispered.

Father patted her back. "How could it possibly be your fault?"

Alia sighed. "Forget it."

"Go on, tell me."

"I got my period at a quarter past eleven," she finally said. "Just when the moon came."

"Oh, darling," said Father. "Things like that don't happen just because you had your period."

"Are you sure?"

Father let out a short laugh. "Of course." He sighed, his breath stirring Alia's hair. "I have no idea what's going on up there, but of this I'm sure."

"I wish I was brave," said Alia. "I wish I wasn't so afraid all the time."

"Bravery isn't not being afraid, love. Bravery is perseverance through fear."

"What?"

"Fancy words," said Father. "It means doing something even though you're afraid. That's what brave is. And you are."

He kissed her forehead and turned out the light. Falling asleep took a long time.

≈≈

Master Bobek stood behind the lectern, his face grey.

"We must remain calm," he said. "You mustn't worry too much. Try to go about your lives as usual. And you are absolutely not allowed to miss school. You have no excuse to stay at home. Everyone will feel better if they carry on as usual. Itti?" He nodded to the boy in the chair next to Alia.

Itti stood, not much taller than when he had been sitting down. "Master Bobek, do you know what really happened?"

The teacher cleared his throat. "We must remain calm," he repeated.

He turned around and pulled down one of the maps from above the blackboard. "Now for today's lesson: bodies of water."

Itti sat down and leaned over. "Your mum," he whispered. "Does she know anything?"

Alia shrugged. "Don't know."

"Can you ask? My parents are moving all our things to the cellar."

She nodded. Itti gave her a quick smile. If Master Bobek had seen the exchange, he said nothing of it, which was unusual for him. Master Bobek concentrated very hard on talking about bodies of water. The children all looked out the windows until Master Bobek swore and drew the curtains.

≈≈

When Alia came home from school, she found the door unlocked. Mother's coat hung on its peg in the hallway.

"Home!" Alia shouted, and took off jacket and shoes and climbed the stairs to the attic.

Mother sat on the balcony, hunched over the telescope's ocular. She was still in her dressing gown, her hair tousled on one side and flat on the other.

Alia forced herself not to look up, but the impossible Moon's cold glow spilled into the upper edge of her vision. "Mother?"

"The level of detail is incredible," Mother mumbled.

Her neck looked dusty, as if she'd been shaking out carpets or going through things in the attic. Alia blew at it and sneezed.

"Have you been out here all day?" Alia wiped her nose on her shirt sleeve.

Mother lifted her gaze from the telescope and turned it to somewhere beyond Alia's shoulder, the same look that Doctor Kazakoff gave visiting children. Grey dust veiled her face; the rings under her eyes were the colour of graphite. Her cheekbones glimmered faintly.

"I suppose I have," she said. "Now off with you, dear. I'm working."

≈≈

The kitchen still smelled of freshly baked bread. On the counter lay a loaf of bread rolled up in a tea towel, next to a bread knife and a jar of honey. Alia unfolded the towel, cut a heel off the loaf and stuffed it in her mouth. It did nothing to ease the burning in her stomach. She turned the loaf over and cut the other heel off. The crust was crunchy and chewy at the same time.

She had eaten her way through most of the loaf when Father spoke behind her. He said her name and put a hand on her shoulder. The other hand gently pried the bread knife from her grip. Then her cheek was pressed against his shirt. Over the slow beat of his heart, Alia could hear the air rushing in and out of his lungs, the faint whistle of breath through his nose. The fire in her belly flickered and died.

"Something's wrong with Mother," she whispered into the shirt.

Father's voice vibrated against her cheek as he spoke. "She's resting now."

≈≈

Alia and her father went about their lives as the President had told them to: going to work, going to school. The classroom emptied as the days went by. Alia's remaining classmates brought rumours of families moving to cellars and caves under the city. The streets were almost deserted. Those who ventured outside did so at a jog, heads bowed between their shoulders. There were no displays of panic or violence. Someone would occasionally burst into tears in the market or on the bus, quickly comforted by bystanders who drew together in a huddle around him.

The radio broadcasts were mostly about nothing, because there was nothing to report. All the scientists and knowledgeable people had established was that the moon didn't seem to affect the earth more than before. It no longer went through phases, staying full and fixed in its position above the city. A respected scientist claimed it was a mirage, and had the city's defence shoot a rocket at it. The rocket hit the moon right where it seemed to be positioned. Burning debris rained back down through the atmosphere for half a day.

As the moon drew closer, it blotted out the midday sun and drowned the city in a ghostly white light, day and night. At sunrise and sundown, the light from the two spheres mixed in a blinding and sickly glare.

Mother stayed on the balcony in her dressing gown, eye to the ocular. Alia heard Father argue with her at night, Father's voice rising and Mother's voice replying in monotone.

Once, a woman in an official-looking suit came to ask Doctor Kazakoff for help. Mother answered the door herself before Father could intercept her. The official-looking woman departed and didn't return.

Alia was still bleeding. She knew you were only supposed to bleed for a few days, but it had been two weeks now. What had started as brownish spotting was now a steady, bright red runnel. It was as if it grew heavier the closer the moon came.

≈≈

Late one night, she heard shouts and the sound of furniture scraping across the floor. Then footsteps came down the stairs; something metallic clattered. Peeking out from her room, Alia saw Father in the hallway with the telescope under one arm.

"This goes out!" he yelled up the stairs. "It's driven you insane!"

Mother came rushing down the stairs, naked feet slapping on the steps. "Pavel Kazakoff, you swine, give it to me." She lunged for the telescope.

Father was heavy and strong, but Mother was furious. She tore the telescope from him so violently that he abruptly let go, and when the telescope crashed into the wall she lost her grip. The floor shook with the telescope's impact. In the silence that followed, Father slowly raised a hand. The front of Mother's dressing gown had opened. He drew it aside.

"Vera." His voice was almost a whisper. "What happened to you?"

In the light from the hallway sconce, Mother's skin was patterned in shades of grey. Uneven rings overlapped each other over her shoulders and arms. The lighter areas glowed with reflected light.

Mother glanced at Father, and then at Alia where she stood gripping the frame of her bedroom door.

"It's regolith," Mother said in a matter-of-fact voice.

She returned upstairs. She left the telescope where it lay.

≈≈

A doctor arrived the morning after. Father gave Alia the choice of staying in her room or going over to Itti's. She chose the latter, hurrying over the courtyard and up the stairs to where Itti lived with his parents.

Itti let her into a flat that was almost completely empty. They passed the kitchen, where Mrs Botkin was canning vegetables, and shut themselves in Itti's room. He only had a bed and his box of comics. They sat down on the bed with the box between them.

"Mother's been making preserves for days now," said Itti.

Alia leafed through the topmost magazine without really looking at the pictures. "What about your father?"

Itti shrugged. "He's digging. He says the cellar doesn't go deep enough."

"Deep enough for what?"

"For, you know." Itti's voice became small. "For when it hits."

Alia shuddered and put the magazine down. She walked over to the window. The Botkin's apartment was on the top floor, and Alia could see right into her own kitchen window across the yard. Her parents were at the dinner table, across from a stranger who must be the doctor. They were discussing something. The doctor leaned forward over the table, making slow gestures with his hands. Mother sat back in her chair, chin thrust out in her Doctor Kazakoff stance. After a while, the physician rose from his chair and left. He emerged from the door to the yard moments later; Alia could see the large bald patch on his head. The physician tilted his head backward and gave the sky a look that seemed almost annoyed. He turned around and hurried out the front gate.

≈≈

Father was still in the kitchen when Alia came home. He blew his nose in a tea towel when he noticed Alia in the doorway.

"Vera is ill," he said. "But we have to take care of her here at home. There's no room at the hospital."

Alia scratched at an uneven spot in the doorjamb. "Is she crazy?"

Father sighed. "The doctor says it's a nervous breakdown, and that it's brought on some sort of skin condition." He cleared his throat and crumpled the tea towel in his hands. "We need to make sure she eats and drinks properly. And that she gets some rest."

Alia looked at her hand, which was gripping the doorjamb so hard the nails were white and red. A sudden warmth spread between her legs as a new trickle of blood emerged.

Father turned the radio on. The announcer was incoherent, but managed to convey that the moon was approaching with increased speed.

≈≈

Mother's dressing gown lay in a heap on the chair next to the balcony door. Mother herself lay naked on the balcony, staring into the sky, a faint smile playing across her face. Alia could see the great wide sea across her chest, and the craters making rings around it. All of the moon's scarred face was sculpted in relief over Mother's body. The crater rims had begun to rise up above the surface.

Alia couldn't make herself step out onto the balcony. Instead, she went down to the courtyard and looked up into the sky. The moon covered the whole square of sky visible between the houses, like a shining ceiling. It had taken on a light of its own, a jaundiced shade of silver. More blood trickled down between Alia's legs.

With the burning rekindling in her stomach, Alia saw how obvious it was. It was all her fault, no matter what Father said. Something had happened when she started bleeding, some power had emerged in her that she wasn't aware of, that drew the moon to her like a magnet. And Mother, so sensitive to the skies and the planets, had been driven mad by its presence. There was only one thing to do. She had to save everyone. The thought filled her with a strange mix of terror and anticipation.

≈≈

Father was on the couch in the living room, leafing through an old photo album. He said nothing when Alia came in and wrapped her arms around him, just leaned his head on her arm and laid his long hand over hers. She detached herself and walked up the stairs to the attic. Mother was as Alia had left her, spread out like a starfish.

Alia crouched beside her still form. "I know why you're ill."

Mother's bright eyes rolled to the side and met Alia's gaze.

"I'll make you well again," Alia continued. "But you won't see me again." Moisture dripped from her eyes into the crater on Mother's left shoulder, and pooled there.

Mother's eyes narrowed.

"Goodbye." Alia bent down and kissed her cheek. It tasted of dust and sour ashes.

≈≈

The plain spread out beyond the city, dotted here and there by clumps of trees. The autumn wind coming in from the countryside was laden with the smell of windfallen fruit and bit at Alia's face. The moonlight leached out the colour from the grass. The birds, if any birds remained here, were quiet. There was only the whisper of grass on Alia's trouser legs, and an underlying noise like thunder. And the moon was really approaching fast, just like the radio man had said: a glowing plain above pressed down like a stony cloud cover. The sight made Alia's face hot with a shock that spread to her ears and down her chest and back, pushing the air out of her lungs. She had a sudden urge to crouch down and dig herself into the ground. The memory of her mother on the balcony flashed by; her body immobile under the regolith, her despairing eyes. Bravery was perseverance through fear. Alia took another step, and her legs, though shaking, held. She could still breathe somehow.

≈≈

When Alia could no longer see the city behind her, a lone hill rose from the plain. It was the perfect place. She climbed the hill step by slow step. The inside of her trousers had soaked through with blood that had begun to cool against her skin, the fabric rasping wetly as she walked. At the top of the hill, she lay down and made herself stare straight up. Why did they always describe fear as cold? Fear was searing hot, burning a hole through her stomach, eating through her lungs.

She forced out a whisper. "Here I am," she told the moon. "I did this. Take me now, do what you're supposed to."

Alia closed her eyes and fought to breathe. The muscles in her thighs tingled and twitched. The vibration in her chest rose in volume, and she understood what it was: the sound of the moon moving through space, the music of the spheres.

≈≈

She had no sensation of time passing. Maybe she'd fainted from fear or bleeding; the sound of footsteps up a hillside woke her. She opened her eyes. Mother stood over her, the terrain across her body in sharp relief against the glowing surface above. The whites of her eyes glistened in twin craters. She held the broken telescope in one hand.

"Go home." Mother's voice was dull and raspy.

Alia shook her head. "It's my fault. I have to make everything okay again."

Mother cocked her head. "Go home, child. This isn't about you. It was never about you. It's my moon."

She grabbed Alia's arm so hard it hurt, and dragged her to her feet. "It was always my moon. Go home."

Mother didn't stink anymore. She smelled like dust and rocks. Her collarbones had become miniature mountain ranges.

Alia pulled her arm out of her mother's grasp. "No."

Mother swung the telescope at her head.

≈≈

The second round of waking was to a world that somehow tilted. Alia opened her eyes to a mess of bright light. Vomit rose up through her throat. She rolled over on her side and retched. When her stomach finally stopped cramping, she slowly sat up. Her brain seemed to slide around a little in her skull.

She was sitting at the foot of the hill. Over her, just a few metres it seemed, an incandescent desert covered the sky.

The moon had finally arrived.

≈≈

Afterward, when Father found her, and the moon had returned to its orbit, and the hill was empty, and everyone pretended that the city had been in the grip of some kind of temporary collective madness, Alia refused to talk about what happened, where Mother had gone. About Mother on the top of the hill, where she stood naked and laughing with her hands outstretched toward the moon's surface. About how she was still laughing as it lowered itself toward the ground, as it pushed her to her knees, as she finally lay flat under its monstrous weight. How she quieted only when the moon landed, and the earth rang like a bell.

70

WHISPERS IN THE MIST

Ray Cluley

Fenton brought the rain in with him along with a gust of drizzle and cold evening air. He shut the door quickly and shook the worst of the weather off, disturbing those sitting at the bar enough to look him over but not so much they scowled at him. It was a cozy little pub. Small, with a low ceiling and dark, dark beams, brass on the stone walls, all of it. Real, too. There was even an open fire, and a dog stretched out in front of it. The older men sitting at the bar wore flat caps and body warmers, their Wellington boots crusty with mud. It was quaint.

Before asking for directions, before checking his phone for signal, Fenton ordered himself a pint. He usually drank lager but this time he ordered one of the regional ales, wanting something thick and heavy, and if it helped ingratiate him with the locals then so much the better. He ordered one named after the pub itself, Old Sexton.

"Here you are, my love."

The woman who took his money looked too young to be using 'my love' colloquially, nineteen or twenty, but Fenton smiled and said thanks. He checked his phone for a signal as he waited for his change. Three bars. Best he'd had anywhere for a while.

"Here you are," the girl said again, handing him his change. A tattoo of flowers spiralled up her wrist. She wore a necklace and earrings that appeared to be made of tin. She looked a bit like Jenny, only a little younger.

"Thanks." He sipped his drink.

"Come off the road have you?"

"Something like that," Fenton said. He licked the foam from his lips and took another sip. It was delicious.

"Thought so. Plenty do that don't live here, especially when the mist's in."

One of the men at the bar looked at him, looked at the girl, and nodded as if confirming her assessment. He held his pint like it was a hot drink, both hands around it as if for warmth. He didn't say anything.

"There's a double bend because o' the Byford property cuttin' into the moors," the barmaid said, "Bet you came off there."

"Well, I—"

"You'd have made one of the corners then come off onto gravel and mud, most likely. Used to be a ditch but Gill filled it in because of all the people coming off there all the time. Didn't you, Gill?"

Gill was a bearded man at the far end of the bar who agreed without knowing what he agreed to, and without caring.

"We got some dangerous roads round 'ere. A little boy was killed only a couple of weeks ago." She tried smiling to lift the sombre mood she'd accidentally created and said, "Put your hazards on I hope?"

"I wasn't driving. I was taking a walk across the moors and lost my way a bit."

Even with the torch, keeping to the path had been difficult. He'd found the road by chance, really, and finding the pub had been another happy accident.

"Walkin' in the dark?"

"Well it wasn't dark when I left. I've come from Bridlecombe."

She raised her eyebrows. "That's quite a way off. You got a long walk heading back that way."

"Yeah, I thought as much. I've heard there's a B&B around here somewhere, The Moorlands? I don't suppose I'm anywhere near it?"

He knew the answer before she said it. "Sorry." She asked the men at the bar but they shook their heads or mumbled, "No, not 'ere."

"Shit."

She smiled at him. "Round here you have to say 'manure'," and she moved down the bar to pick up some empties. "There's a number for a taxi by the phone."

Fenton thanked her, though he wouldn't use the number, and took his drink over to a table by the fire. He'd just rest for a moment and then head back out. The dog, a black and white collie, lifted its head to look him over and sniff his feet as he passed, then settled down again with a huffed sigh as if Fenton was a disappointment.

Someone had spilled something on the table where Fenton sat. He righted the glass and grouped the table mats over the worst of the spill, watching it soak into the cardboard. He knew the feeling; his coat was supposed to be waterproof but it must have reached its saturation point because it clung to him now as a shiny sodden skin. He took it off to drape over a chair facing the fire. His long-sleeved shirt clung to him and was properly wet at the neck and shoulders. Not that it was really raining out, as such. It was one of those drizzles that sort of just sat in the air somehow without going anywhere. He wondered if it would turn into fog or mist for his walk back.

He watched his coat create a mist of its own, steaming as it dried.

"All right?"

A young man in a rugby jumper with a handful of toilet tissue in one hand approached the table. He didn't do it very steadily.

"Hello," Fenton said.

The man pointed to the table with his handful of tissue and said, "Spilt my drink."

"Oh, sorry," said Fenton, getting up, "I didn't know you were sitting here."

The man raised his hand and said, "No bother," before dabbing at what was left of the spill. "No, really, sit down. I was just going."

The man mopped at the table and crammed the damp tissue into his empty glass, knocked it – "Whoops!" – and though he tried to grab it, all he did was knock Fenton's glass as well, which tilted its contents into his lap. Both of them grabbed at the pint to set it straight but they were too late to save much of it.

73

"Sorry mate."

Fenton stood and wiped at his trousers. They were already soaked through anyway. "Don't worry about it. Been one of those days."

One of those years.

"No, I'm really sorry." The man laughed, adding, "And a bit of a clumsy bastard."

You're pissed, that's why, Fenton wanted to say.

"Dee, get us another pint of what he was drinking."

"Really, it's okay," said Fenton, happy with what he still had left, but again the man had his hand up—no bother—and went to the bar.

Fenton wondered if it was a sign, proof that he shouldn't have stopped yet. Then again, if it was a sign, maybe it meant he was supposed to stay a while longer. Bloody signs and superstitions. Jenny would know, what with her ley lines and coffin rocks and stone circles.

"Dee says you've walked all the way from Bridlecombe."

Rugby shirt was back, with another pint of ale for Fenton and a lager for himself. He sat down at the table, said, "Cheers," and made as if to clink Fenton's glass with his before exaggerating a change of mind and pulling it back to avoid another spill. He laughed, and guzzled half his drink down.

"Yeah," said Fenton. "I was just about to head back, actually." He tried to guzzle a good amount as well so he could leave, but the ale was heavy and creamy and difficult to swallow quickly. More of a dessert than a drink.

"Long way to come for a pint," said his new friend.

Fenton did his best to smile back politely.

"I'm goin' to get a taxi after this," said the man, "Dee won't let me drive now."

Too bloody right, Fenton thought.

"You want to share it?"

"Thanks," said Fenton, "but I'll probably walk."

"Walk? It'll be too dark, mate."

"I've got a torch."

"Won't help you with the fog, though."

"Fog?"

Fenton turned to look out of the window but all he

saw was a picnic table at the edge of a small car park. Saw it clearly.

"Well, maybe not now. But they'll be whisperin' tonight, I bet."

Fenton was bringing his drink up for another go at swallowing as much of it as he could but stopped before the glass was at his mouth. "Sorry?"

"Oh, I'm Terry."

The man had clearly misunderstood the question but Fenton shook the hand he offered anyway and said his own name.

"Fenton," Terry repeated. "You from round here? Originally I mean? Name like that, sounds like you should be from round here. Fenton of the fen."

"I'm from the city."

"Oh. Right."

The man turned his attention to the silent television above the bar. The weather girl was on with a large colourful map behind her. It was all lines and arrows and sweeping hand movements. She looked a bit like Jenny.

"I'd love to give *her* a heavy shower," Terry said, raising his glass to the silent TV. He turned back to Fenton and said, "Eh? Make her temperature rise, eh? Eh?"

Fenton gave a tight-lipped smile.

"You gay?"

"No."

Terry raised his hands. "It's okay if you are."

Fenton gave his same tight-lipped smile.

"You like rugby?"

Fenton shook his head. "No. What did you mean by "they'll be whisperin' tonight" just now?"

"What?"

"Just now. When we were talking about the fog. You said they'll be whispering."

"Oh. Well, them's in the mist. Whisperin'." He cracked a smile as if it were a private joke between them, or as if he were merely humouring him like he would a child asking a silly question. "You know, walking the ghost lines to the coffin stone? *Wooooh.*" He waggled his fingertips at Fenton. "Yeah, they'll be whisperin' tonight for sure," said Terry, "Won't they, Gill?"

Gill nodded, watching the silent TV. Fenton wondered if he was only watching it as way to ignore Terry.

Fenton excused himself and went to the bar.

"Mine's a lager, Fenton mate. Cheers."

Fenton opened his mouth to say something, hesitated, and changed his mind.

"Terry's not bothering you, is he?" Dee asked.

Fenton hesitated just long enough that she'd know yes, he was, before saying, "No, he's all right. I don't suppose you're still serving food?"

She smiled an awkward apology at him. "Sorry."

Fenton said, 'Manure,' and was pleased to make her laugh even if she wasn't Jenny.

"Don't serve that neither," she said, and Fenton surprised himself by laughing too. "We've got plenty of crisps or nuts?"

Terry was turned around in his seat to face them, frowning. "*What* did you say?"

"Oh Terry, shush."

But Terry stood, his chair toppling behind him. The dog by the fire barked once and was quiet but Terry blustered on. "Nuts, am I? Is that what's so funny?"

"Nobody said that," Dee said. "Sit down, you're being silly."

"Do you want another drink?" Fenton tried.

"No he doesn't," said Dee. "Terry, why don't you get back now, eh?"

"Give me my keys, then."

"I'll call you a taxi."

"*You're* a taxi," Terry said, without cracking a smile. He stumbled over the fallen chair and grabbed a jacket from a peg by the door. "Come on, Sally."

The dog leapt to its feet and rushed to do as it was told, claws scratching against the stone floor as it scrambled to Terry's side. A gust of cold evening air came in with the open door and then they were gone.

"Don't mind Terry. He's a bit of an idiot when he's had a few."

"And he's always had a few," said one of the older men, and the others chuckled quietly into their drinks.

"He said something about people whispering," said

Fenton. "In the fog."

Dee shrugged. Gill said, "Mist."

"Sorry?"

"Fog is thicker, can't see much." He took a long gulp from his glass, draining it for a dramatic pause. "When they whisper, they whisper in the mist."

"Who?"

Gill went to take another gulp, then made a show of realizing his glass was empty. Cunning bugger.

Fenton asked Dee to top him up as well, and of course the other men at the bar gave him some attention then so he bought them drinks too. It didn't matter. Besides, perhaps they'd chip in with a detail or two themselves once Gill got going. He bought himself another ale, deciding it would be his last. He was supposed to be cutting down and already this was number three. Well, two and a half.

"Cold air of the evenin' sinks down," said one of the other men as Dee poured their glasses full. He made a gesture with both hands. "And condensation puts water in the air, makes mist. Like clouds, only on the ground, see."

"That's right, that's right, but you gets it at night, too," said the other.

"You're both right," said Dee, and they smiled at her for it. Or maybe they smiled because she'd put two more drinks in front of them. "This is Seeton and this is Lloyd. You know Gill. Anyway, it's the moors. It's always cold and wet."

They toasted her point, happy to leave it at that.

Fenton didn't want to let it go just yet, though. "What about these whisperers, then?"

"It's a local legend," Gill said. "You're not local, are you?"

"No."

"Not even country."

"Not really."

"Hm."

Fenton waited.

"Round here, sometimes the roads are dangerous," Gill explained. "Like with the poor boy got hit. Sometimes the moors are what's dangerous, like with that tourist who died of hypothermia. Sometimes, working on a farm or such, that's dangerous too. I've got too many examples of those."

"Okay."

"Has to be, don't it? That's life. Sometimes people die, and that's life too."

Fenton said nothing. He didn't want to encourage this kind of talk. He wanted to hear about the whisperers in the mist.

"Everything ends," Gill said. "But around here, they don't always move on. Sometimes they stay."

Fenton looked at the other men for an agreement but Lloyd was looking into the creamy head of his pint and Seeton was watching the TV. Dee, sat on a stool behind the bar, was texting. Fenton noticed her nails were painted but only at the tips. Jenny used to do that.

"So these whisperers in the mist, they're ghosts then?"

Gill shrugged. "Might be. Might be they *are* the mist."

"Right."

Gill shook his head. "It's just stories," he said, but Fenton could tell he didn't mean it.

"Is it only locals who hear them? Is it only locals who whisper? Those bound to the land the mist touches?"

Gill looked him over, a proper up and down this time, and said, "You've heard this already."

Dee chipped in without looking up from her phone. "Terry said something."

"I've heard it before," Fenton admitted.

"Then you know."

"Sometimes, people hear whispers," Fenton said. "Voices. In the mist. Sometimes people call to them but all they do is whisper.   That's all I know, really."

"Sometimes," Gill agreed. "Sometimes, when the mist's in, you can hear them right outside your window. Right outside your front door. And you might recognize it, too. The voice might be someone you know. Someone you knew."

A hush had descended, a quiet that was somehow different to the silent TV. The fire crackle seemed muted and Dee paused in tapping at her phone.

"Do people ever see them?" Fenton asked.

"There's a few say they have."

"But don't go *following* them," said Seeton, "They'll lead you along the ghost walk and into a bog, or off a ledge, or into a river. Into trouble, anyways."

"You're thinking of will-o'-the-wisp," said Gill, with a dismissive wave of his hand.

Fenton wiped froth from his lips. His pint was nearly gone again. He barely remembered drinking it.

"They're not dangerous," said Gill. "The lost can only hurt you by not being there."

"Lost? As in missing? Or lost, dead?"

Gill shrugged, "One leads t'other round here." He frowned. "Who told you about them?"

Fenton was tempted to say it was Terry but thought this man would know a lie. "My girlfriend told me," he said. "She was from round here."

Dee looked up, briefly intrigued.

"She told me all sorts of stories. The ley lines of power, coffin stones that cracked if you were going to die that year. Whispers in the mist. She said if you heard them, they'd tell you all you've ever done wrong."

"Well, could be she's right about that. Way I was told it, though, going back a few years mind, was them's in the mist are lonely."

"Lonely?"

"Yeah, lonely. Ghosts get lonely too, I should think. That's why they call to their loved ones. Or *any*one, probably. Only, being dead, and in the mist, their voices don't carry much. Not everyone hears it. Ones who knew 'em have the best chance. Or if you're nearby. Got to be very close, mind."

Fenton nodded. There was a kind of sense to it. For a ghost story. If they even *were* ghosts. Knowing he'd be going back out there soon, he hoped they weren't.

When Gill said nothing else, Fenton asked, "Have *you* heard them?"

One of the others inhaled deeply. Dee returned to her texting. Gill drained the last of his drink and looked into the empty glass. Fenton wondered if he was hinting for another, and was about to ask for one, when the man suddenly excused himself from the bar. "Two pints in, two pints out," he said, and went to the gents.

When he was gone, Seeton said, "Yeah, he's heard

them. Lost his wife a while ago."

"Mary," said Lloyd, raising what was left of his glass to her. "Bless her."

"He hears her sometimes when the mist's in, so he says, but he doesn't listen if he can help it. Comes here instead."

"He's better than the weathergirl. If he's in 'ere then there'll be mist out *there*."

"This evening, then?"

Fenton looked from man to man, then to Dee who was smiling up from her mobile. She wasn't like Jenny at all. She didn't believe any of them.

Fenton wanted to. He had to. It all sounded a bit *Wuthering Heights* or whatever, ghosts at the windows and lost on the moors, but if he believed, then there was a chance for him and Jenny.

"Well, thank you gentlemen," he said, retrieving his jacket from where it had dried by the fire. He put it on over his damp shirt, glad of its warmth, and zipped it up to his chin. "I'll be heading back out now."

"Call a taxi," Dee suggested again.

"I'm alright walking, really." He plucked his new coat away from his skin then raised one foot to show his new walking boots. "It's why I came here."

Gill returned from the toilet as Fenton was opening the front door. "You lost anyone?" he asked.

Fenton felt the chill of outside wrapping around him. "Yeah."

"The one told you the story," said Gill. "The one from round 'ere."

Fenton merely nodded.

"Stay and have another pint," Gill said.

But Fenton said no, thanks, and stepped out into the cold evening air.

≈≈

The car park was clear but a mist was indeed forming. It had settled into a dip where the road descended in a gentle slope. Fenton was soon enveloped by shreds of low cloud clinging to his ankles and then his shins, tossed away as he walked, turning in slow spirals as he passed through. There was very little by way of a footpath here, so he walked right at the road edge, as close as he could to the verge without stepping off into the moors. He could always step further away from the road if he saw the glow of headlights, but he wondered how clear they'd be further down, in the valley. He'd seen how fast people drove in the country and he didn't think the night, or a little mist, would slow them down much.

To either side, open land stretched for miles with little but the occasional line of hedgerow to mark a border of some sort, but he only knew that from memory; he could see very little of it now. He knew that to his right the land would rise again eventually to some tor or another, and he knew that there was a camp site not very far the other way which he could cut across, but he decided to follow the road for a while.

It was a clear night, at least. He wondered if it had to be, in order for mist to form. There were so many stars out here, away from the streetlights and the shop signs of the city. A sprawling mass of constellations scattered across the sky, each with a strange name and a function, probably, pointing him north or east or whatever. He didn't know much about the outdoors. He was a townie, that's what Jenny said. Closest he got to a field was playing football at the weekend, and the only trees he knew were the ones lining the more suburban streets of his neighbourhood. He'd never seen the moors until now. Jenny had been right, there *was* a desolate beauty to them and they were practically on his doorstep, not much more than a two hour drive. He should have accompanied her at least once when she visited family. Now Jenny was gone and he had no idea what to do with his life. "You need to figure out what you want," she'd said. They were pretty much her last words.

A withered bunch of flowers had been tied to a post to his right where the road branched. Or rather, a beautiful bunch of flowers had been tied there that had since withered. The heads were dark and drooping on stems that had curled. Fenton knew how they felt. Another bunch had been left on the ground but whatever shape had held them together was now gone and they lay scattered. He knew how that felt, too. Someone had no doubt lost a loved one here, perhaps in a car accident. It seemed likely—the road forked in a dip where mist gathered. Maybe they'd crashed their vehicle. Maybe they'd been struck by one. He remembered the boy they'd told him about in the pub.

He wondered if he'd hear the boy whisper. He listened, but heard nothing.

How much time had to pass first? He'd lost Jenny only a month ago, but it felt like so much longer. She'd know how long to wait. She knew all sorts about ghosts and superstitions and ancient places and he had teased her for it without ever believing. Now he missed those stupid stories. He missed everything about her. He missed holding her, undressing her. She liked to wear vest tops and long skirts, cheap jewellery like the tin things the barmaid had been wearing. Her perfume was one of sandalwood or jasmine, scents which still clung to everything in his flat. He missed her voice, the way she said his name, the gentle west country accent he would mock; his little hobbit girl. She'd exaggerated that accent when telling him about the whisperers in the mist. He wanted to hear it again. He listened for it, treading carefully, his footsteps muffled by the soft mulch of ground underfoot. Smothered by the mist.

The mist was heavier now, no longer breaking away from his legs as he walked but swirling around them, between them. Perhaps it hoped to slow him down, hold him forever in its shifting shape.

Fenton heard a sigh.

Wondering if he'd made the sound himself, lost in thoughts of Jenny, he held his breath. He listened.

There was a voice.

It was a low voice: wordless, but rising and falling as if with speech.

A pause. A silence.

He thought perhaps this mist was fog now because there was so much of it, then remembered what that old man Seeton had said in the pub, that it was all down to thickness. Fenton could still just about see, such as the stand of trees up ahead. Unless they *weren't* trees…

There it was again. A voice. Unless the mist distorted sound, it came from the upright shapes ahead. Perhaps the dead wandered the moors in groups, whispering their chill chorus to any who would listen.

"Come on," the voice said. "Your turn." There was a soft sing-song quality to it.

Then quiet again. Was he meant to reply?

"Hello?"

Speaking gave Fenton the courage to move forward, towards the figures, and he did so at a rush, eager to see, eager to ask them about the others.

Terry turned from one of the trees, zipping himself up, just as his dog squatted to let off a stream of her own.

"Fenton of the fen! Bloody hell! You scared me, mate. I thought you was a ghost, coming out of the fog like that."

"Mist," Fenton said. He looked around but there was only the dog. Sally.

"Keep losing her out here, but I left the leash at the pub. You might get lost yourself if you're not careful." Terry said it with friendly concern, not as a threat; whatever animosity had existed between them back at the pub seemed forgotten.

Fenton held up his torch.

"Won't do much good turned off. You *trying* to get lost?"

Lost my way a while ago, Fenton wanted to say. Lost myself in Jenny, and again when she was gone.

"I'll walk with you a bit," Terry said. He belched into his fist.

"It's okay, I—"

"Sally, come on. Let's go."

The dog was little more than a dark movement beneath the mist, churning it with the upright arc of her wagging tail. To Fenton, it was like looking at a boat from underneath, the curls of mist like water in which the rudder of something furry steered its course. It was rather disorientating.

"She's all I've got now," said Terry. He cast a look at Fenton which he probably thought was sly, but Fenton saw it. "We wander around together, forever, haunting the mists. Calling out for those who knew us."

"I think I'll go cross country," said Fenton, "Take a short cut."

But Terry grabbed his arm. "I'm just joking with you!"

"Right."

"I'm not a ghost, mate."

No shit.

"I mean, come on. We just had a pint. I have a dog. What kind of ghost has a dog?"

The dead get lonely.

"There's no such thing as ghosts anyway," said Terry. "It's all bullshit. All of it. Except aliens, *maybe*."

Fenton wondered how Jenny could stand it when he doubted her. She so much wanted to believe. It must have been hard telling her stories and seeing him not even listening. Not really.

"There's supposed to be a bed and breakfast around here," Fenton said, "I'm looking for The Moorlands?"

Terry shrugged. "Moorlands everywhere, mate."

The tail-rudder before them dipped under the mist for a moment, then cut a quick trail through it, hurrying away.

"Sally, heel!"

But the tail-rudder was moving ahead, disappearing into the mist.

"Sally! Come back! Don't leave me, girl."

Fenton wondered if anyone else was near to hear Terry's disembodied voice. He wondered what they'd make of it, hearing it in the dark weather calling for someone, telling her to stay. Would it become a story to tell over a pint or two down the Old Sexton?

Terry moved ahead to catch up with his dog but Fenton stopped walking. Then he began moving backwards, lengthening the distance between them quickly and quietly. He didn't want to listen to Terry prattle on. He didn't want to be distracted.

He stepped off the road onto the soft ground of the moors. Beside him was a tangle of hedgerow and a few boards of a half-hearted fence. Terry was only a shadow ahead. Fenton took another step back, slowly, and crouched beside the hedge, hoping to lose his silhouette against it.

"Sally? Fuck sake. Stick your torch on, mate, I can't— Fenton?"

Fenton remained quiet. He even considered lying

down but then Sally barked and Terry followed the sound into the dark, calling her name. A few more minutes and he'd probably forget meeting Fenton again, drunk as he was.

The ground was springy beneath Fenton's feet, rich with the wet smell of earth. The thin vapour around him was aglow with moonlight and everything smelled fresh and clean and alive. He was reminded that Jenny'd wanted them to make love outdoors some time. In the heath, she'd said, in the open countryside beneath the stars, and he'd said he would, but they never did. And now they probably never would.

"Oh Jenny," he said. "Where are you?"

Fenton stood and tried to get his bearings. He could still make out the road, but following it would only lead him back to the pub. He could take it to where the road forked, but he thought if anyone whispered there it would be the one who'd been struck down. He imagined the figure, a small boy-shadow standing in the dark with wreaths of mist coiling about his shins, mouth opening and closing with hushed sounds Fenton could barely hear.

Jenny had not been struck by a car. He would not find her on the road.

He stepped over a fallen fence board and began to trek across the open ground.

"Jenny," he said, quietly.

He didn't know where she was now. She had always gone home on her own for visits. She'd asked him to come with her lots of times but he'd always been too busy, coming up with an excuse not to go. She was asking him to visit because she'd seen something serious between them, but he hadn't heard that in the invite until it was too late. Until she'd stopped asking. If he'd gone with her, if he'd come to bloody Dartmoor *then*, things never would have gone wrong between them, he was sure of that. If he'd only listened...

He listened now. He strained to hear her, hoping what he knew of her, what he'd lost, would call to him somehow. Her family ran a B&B called The Moorlands. It was around here somewhere. Somewhere where the mist whispered and ghosts walked, where stones stood in circles and hills hid fairy halls and buried dead…

Christ, there were a hundred such places.

He ripped at the Velcro of his waterproof pocket, found his phone and thumbed down to her name even though he knew he shouldn't. He'd call her. He'd said he wouldn't, but he would, and he'd explain where he was, how far he'd come to be with her again, and that he wasn't very drunk at all, barely tipsy. And this time *she'd* have to listen.

He had a signal. Only one bar, but it was enough.

He wondered if she'd changed the ringtone. Wondered if she'd even kept his number. She must have, surely, if only to know it was him calling.

"Fenton," she said.

"Hello Jenny."

"You promised."

"I know, I know, but I miss you, Jen. Don't you miss me?"

"Fenton…"

"It could be better this time. I even came to Devon, you know, like I said I would? Do you remember what you said about the heath? We could do that now. I'm here, Jenny. I came down to—"

"Fenton, you're not listening to me. You never lis-"

"Jenny, I just want—"

"You have to stop doing this. It's over."

"Jenny, we're —"

"—breaking up—"

"Jenny?"

"—mised—"

Promised? Missed?

Mist?

"Jenny?"

His phone died. The display was still lit but the signal symbol was gone. He backtracked a few steps, eyes down on the phone, waiting for a bar, just one line of signal. His thumb was poised over the call button, her name still on screen.

"*Fuck*ing *phone*. Come-on-come-on-come-on."

He wiped the mist from his face, from his eyes. He shook his mobile, pressed call anyway, but all it did was flash a message that told him he'd failed.

The pub had a signal. He'd go back there and call.

But the road was gone. He turned, looking, but the moors were all around. In the past, people would put a light in a particular window to guide lost travellers. There was nothing like that now. Fenton walked in a strange limbo, clouds at his feet and the sky above freckled with stars. He stumbled in the dark, trying his phone, "Jenny?" but knowing he'd never find a way back. "Jenny..."

Her name came from his mouth as a shred of vapour, and as he spoke he shrouded himself with apologies and promises to her. They drifted from his lips as mist and trailed behind him, obscuring the way he had come, hiding the way forward. But he kept trying, ignoring their lost connection.

"Jenny..."

He spoke until nothing was clear anymore, moving through the mist he'd made with each of his excuses, rambling as the weather buried him. He missed her more than he could explain, but he tried, and somewhere in the night a lost chorus echoed his despair. He gave his voice to it, walking and talking until taken by the mist and moors, searching for someone, somewhere, to belong. Drifting in the dark, crying softly:

"Jenny..."

A WOMAN'S PLACE

TOPOGRAPHY AND ENTRAPMENT IN CHARLOTTE PERKINS GILMAN'S 'THE YELLOW WALLPAPER'

V.H. Leslie

The end of the nineteenth century saw the emergence of the 'New Woman,' women who wanted to work and take an active part in politics and social change. They felt that the role of women shouldn't be defined by marriage and childbirth. In fact many New Women advocated 'free unions' whereby men and women could enter into monogamous relationships without the bonds of matrimony. The New Woman was seen as the equivalent of the decadent man, the dandy; a figure obsessed with aestheticism and excess. They were seen as dangerous and degenerative challenging conventional ideas about gender. The fin de siècle, or the end of the century, witnessed a blurring of gender boundaries where masculinity and femininity were being radically redefined.

Much of the literature of the 1890s focused on this new kind of heroine challenging their place in society, often addressing themes like marital discord, female sexuality and madness. But the fin de siècle also saw an increase in the women behind the fictionalization, the writers themselves. Work by women writers flooded the market as they contributed to fashionable magazines and periodicals. These new writers opted for a relatively new genre as their weapon of choice to attack societal norms; the short story became an apt vehicle for women writers to expose the anxieties of the age and to highlight their concerns. The length of the short story allowed writers to express ideas concisely, symbolically and allegorically whilst reaching a larger readership in publications such as *The Savoy* and *The Yellow Book*. What emerged from this fertile period were the seeds of feminism that would grow into a literature spanning generations to come.

A ROOM OF ONE'S OWN

'The Yellow Wallpaper' is about a woman suffering from some kind of mental or emotional breakdown, the causes of which are never fully explained. In order to alleviate her condition, her husband, a physician, decides to rent a property in the countryside as part of her Rest Cure Treatment. The story begins outside the house but the narrator voices her concerns in the first few lines noting, 'something queer' about the building. Gothic tropes are used to describe the building, first as a 'hereditary estate' then as a 'haunted house' to set the scene for supernatural possibilities and hint at something monstrous within. As if the reader is moving closer to the property, we are introduced to the garden, comprising of orderly 'box-bordered paths' and 'long-grape covered arbors' as well as 'hedges and walls and gates that lock' suggesting that the outdoors is cultivated and contained whilst also introducing ideas of imprisonment and entrapment.

As the reader moves over the threshold and into the house, the narrator confides that she would have preferred to rent the room downstairs that opens up onto the garden. Her preference to be close to nature is all the more poignant when her husband insists they take the attic room at the top of the house. We learn that the room used to be a nursery and then a playroom. The bars on the windows, seemingly a protective measure, continues the semantic field of incarceration, as does the fact that the beds are strapped down.

We learn that the narrator is not only imprisoned within the house but also in her marriage. Her husband John does not believe his wife's assertions that she is seriously sick and diagnoses her as suffering from a, 'temporary nervous depression—a hysterical tendency.' As part of her treatment she takes a variety of modern medicine cures from 'phosphates' and 'tonics' but she is absolutely prohibited to 'work.' Nineteenth century attitudes to neurological conditions were very different. John seems to attribute his wife's hysterical tendencies to mental exertion, such as writing and socializing. His cure is essentially enforced seclusion.

The narrator has a very different opinion about what would 'cure' her; 'I believe congenial work, with excitement and change, would do me good.' Despite the rules imposed by her husband she does indeed write, albeit in secret. The narrative itself functions as a rebellion against her husband and society's demands. Gilman seems to suggest that female literary proficiency and creativity is dangerous to patriarchal values. The story can therefore be interpreted as a woman's struggle for artistic as well as physical freedom and independence.

MADWOMAN IN THE ATTIC

The attic is a significant physical space as it is far removed from the hub of the home and the outside world, being a location where more extreme possibilities can take place. In Gothic texts, the attic is often where the supernatural finds fruition and arguably there is a haunting of sorts in 'The Yellow Wallpaper.' If we consider a building as a person, the attic is the 'head space' symbolizing the psyche. Considering the bars on the windows and the strapped down beds it could well be that the building was once an asylum. In the text, the narrator's confinement to her attic room is the catalyst that drives the story, developing into a focus on her mental health as it deteriorates.

All the while the narrator is confined her obsession with the room's yellow wallpaper grows. At first it is a dislike of its 'unclean' and 'repellent' colour and then its irregular patterns and 'lame uncertain curves.' The design is not governed by 'symmetry' or 'repetition' but is a random arrangement of shapes. The design of the wallpaper is even described as 'committing suicide' as the angels 'plunge off at outrageous angles,' foreshadowing a possible reading of the narrator's fate.

As the narrator spends more time in the room she becomes convinced the wallpaper conceals something. First she recognizes a 'sub-pattern,' then a shape, before finally discerning the figure of a woman. The woman is 'stooped down and creeping around' indicating that she is subservient. In the day the pattern 'keeps her still' but by moonlight the design transforms to prison bars, the woman behind the paper trapped. It is then that she becomes more active, shaking the pattern in an attempt to get out and the narrator's initial fear of the figure is replaced by a desire to set her free. The narrator cannot determine whether it is one woman or many, possibly suggesting that all women 'creep' submissively behind various social patterns and expectations. As for the narrator herself, the wallpaper represents her autonomous self lurking behind the pretence that is her marriage and her social role. Like a princess in a tower she can see the world below that she is forbidden to enter because the attic prison commands a good view of the surrounding countryside. It has four windows, with very different views from each. One looks out onto the garden below, the first topographical space mentioned perhaps due to its proximity to the house. Although a contained and cultivated landscape initially, it is described later as being 'riotous' and 'mysterious'. Garden spaces are significant as they function as a midway point between the wider world and the home. Though they still belong to the domestic realm, they can also be untamed and wild. As such, the narrator takes solace in the garden but does not venture further than its borders. Other windows command a view of the bay, gateway to the sea, and a view of the road, both offering the possibility of travel. A fourth window looks out onto the countryside itself, a wild space consisting of 'velvet meadows' representing freedom. The windows symbolize different opportunities that the narrator could take, should she be able to find a way out.

The windows also emphasize the significance of perspective. Although the first person perspective naturally encourages us to empathize it is clear that her experiences are the product of a severely depressed state of mind. As her delusions become more manifest, the narrative viewpoint becomes increasingly unreliable and the reader is left to interpret the story's ambiguous ending for themselves. The story culminates with her husband attempting to break down the door of the attic room as he is excluded from what is now a feminine space, only with her permission is he able to gain entry into her insular world. What he finds there is very much up to the reader.

ANGEL OF THE HOUSE

The house was traditionally seen as a feminine space where 'angels' resided over domestic affairs, selfless in their devotion to their husband and children. Indeed Coventry Patmore established the idea of the 'Angel of the House' in his poem of the same name. In 'The Yellow Wallpaper' Gilman explores the importance of the family home and questions not only what it represents but what it conceals. She also considers the consequences of women rebelling against the feminine ideal. However, due to the mental health of the narrator, Gilman forces the reader to make their own minds up about the fate of the heroine. The narrator's final words spoken aloud; "I've got out at last and you can't put me back!" are purposefully ambiguous. It could be seen that the narrator's obsession with the wallpaper has led to madness, so much so that she has assumed the identity of the woman in the paper. Alternatively she could have in fact committed suicide, especially considering she mentions the temptation to 'jump out the window' moments before, literally becoming the ghostly figure that once haunted her. Gilman wrote a short essay 'The Extinct Angel' as a reaction to Patmore's ideal of femininity, in which she proposes that the Angel of the House is dead, which suggests that Gilman had a similar intention for her protagonist here. If Gilman does indeed kill off the narrator, she could be implying that the concept of the submissive woman is obsolete. On the other hand, she could be suggesting that the only way for women to escape the pattern of their lives is through death.

Personally, I favour a more optimistic reading, in which the text champions female solidarity, women working together to escape their manmade prisons. The narrator's final lines merely indicate that she has realized that all women are one and the same, trapped behind social conventions, her final lines a rallying call to a generation of New Women. Recognizing the bonds that constrain you are the first steps to freedom.

Further Reading:
Elaine Showalter *Sexual Anarchy*
Rita Felski *The Gender of Modernity*

THE OTHER BOY

Daniel Mills

We moved to Vermont when I was an infant. My parents were lifelong New Yorkers, but they gave up the lease on their Chelsea apartment to buy a slate-roofed saltbox in the hills east of Hubbardton. We lived in that house from 1983 to 1986, but I was so young at the time that I can't remember much of anything about the interior, except for the ceilings, which dripped during storms, and the crown glass windows in the kitchen that stretched and warped the world beyond, bending the light into knots.

My mother hated it there. In those days, she hated almost everything. One evening, I remember, I ventured onto the back porch and found her sitting in her rocking chair with a shawl draped across her shoulders. From the deck, you could see across the property line to the neighbours' farm: twenty acres of stony pasture sloping to a muddy pond.

At first I thought she was asleep—she was so still— but her eyes were open and fixed on the pond in the distance. I stood there for several minutes, but she didn't look at me or otherwise acknowledge my presence, and the crows screeched and blackened the sky overhead.

Our house lay within walking distance of the Hubbardton battlefield—the site of a minor rear guard action in July 1777 that had served as a prelude to the larger battles of Bennington and Saratoga. This skirmish lasted little more than an hour, but it was re-enacted every year in July when hundreds of men converged on the town. They made camp under the stars and drank rum from pewter cups. On the following morning, they fired blanks from replica muskets and charged each other with blunted bayonets.

We went to the re-enactment once. My father dressed me in a wool coat and tricorn and brought me to watch the battle. This was in 1986, our final summer in Vermont. I was three years old, nearly four, and I suppose I must have wandered off because I found myself alone.

I was in the woods. That is the first thing I remember: the sparkle of green leaves, shadows on the musty earth. The heat was terrible. My legs ached, but the woods went on, and I was too frightened to stop and rest. Eventually I reached the edge of the forest and emerged onto a slope bathed in sunlight.

A line of men marched toward me up the hill, soldiers. They wore red coats and navy blue and moved to the rhythm of a clattering drum, muskets held at their waists. Cannons roared. The earth rumbled. Then came the boom of musketry, shattering the heat-damp air. One of the redcoats dropped, clutching his hands to his chest, while the others broke into a run, shouting as they ascended the ridgeline. I turned and fled away up the slope.

White smoke curled and drifted along the ground. It stung my eyes, blinding me, and I staggered forward with no guide but the crack of gunfire in front of me and the shouts of the men behind. I heard the screams of the wounded, the dying—the sounds all magnified by smoke, looming like ghosts out of the stifling heat.

Then someone was beside me, another boy. He didn't speak but simply grasped my hand and broke into a run, holding me fast so that I stumbled after him through the haze of smoke and sunlight, almost falling. It was all so real—terrifyingly so—and the two of us ran headlong across the pasture, sprinting as the two lines crashed together, like the jaws of a trap out of which we flew, headlong, and sailed into the high grass beyond, panting like dogs as the sun poured down on us and the smoke drifted away over our heads.

My rescuer was a few years older than me. He wore a yellow coat with sleeves that flared at the shoulders. Buttons gleamed on his chest. *GR*, they said. *Georgius Rex*. It was, I later learned, the uniform of a British drummer boy.

The din of battle subsided. We heard birdsong in the trees, robins and finches. The other boy stood and stretched and began to walk. I don't remember anything else about that day. We never returned to the battlefield, and it was only long afterward, when I was in middle school, that I thought to ask my father about the incident.

"Who was he? The boy who found me?"

"Found you?"

"At the re-enactment. When we lived in Vermont."

My father shook his head. "I don't know, Paul," he said, rubbing his eyes so that he didn't have to look at me. "That was all so long ago."

≈≈

We moved back to New York in November 1986. It was my father's idea, I think—his final bid to save his failing marriage, as if the noise and chaos of the city might somehow put to flight whatever awful silence had enveloped my mother, settling over her like wet snow.

And so the years passed, though I did not forget the other boy, not even after I stumbled through adolescence to find myself in the wilds of an unsettled adulthood. Light on green leaves. The battlefield. My mother on the porch with the pond before her—black and motionless, an open eye. The memories returned to me in the moments before sleep, circling the bed on moth-wings before kindling, blazing, fading with the dark.

When I was eighteen, I went away to college in Maine where I studied English literature. I had always been a quiet child, and bookish besides, so it seemed a natural enough choice. Freshman year, my roommate was a baseball player two years my senior. He had a serious girlfriend with whom he spent most nights and I was usually alone in the room.

Winter descended. The darkness drew in and I took to spending my evenings at the library, reading while I listened to music in headphones. I was largely undiscriminating. I read Milton, Plath, Lovecraft, Yeats— whatever might keep me awake and further delay the frigid walk across campus. Inevitably, though, the CD player's batteries ran down and the last disc ceased to spin. The trap closed, and the quiet pressed down on me, pounding in my temples.

The way home followed a wooded path lined with red pine and sodium streetlamps. Sometimes, as I walked past, they would wink off, as though plunged into darkness by my presence, so that I thought of ghosts and childhood and the places beyond memory. Later, lying awake in the morning, I watched the sunlight push through the blinds and recalled the field across which we had run, the two of us, and the loneliness that had followed in our wake.

Finals came and went. I boarded a train and traveled home to the City. My parents had separated some years before, my mother having fallen into a paralyzing depression, and I stayed with my father throughout that summer. By then, he was already ill, the skin stretched over bones as brittle as old scrimshaw. On Sunday mornings, we went to the park together and watched the ducks and the dog-walkers until he grew tired and I brought him home again.

He was seeing another woman, a nurse he had met in the hospital waiting room. Her name was Lisa. She couldn't have been much older than I was, but the age gap didn't seem to bother them. They even joked about it ("my trophy-wife-to-be," he sometimes called her, but only when she was present) and she was indeed beautiful, tall and fair and brown-eyed.

I was jealous of her, I think, and my father too, though I wouldn't have admitted it, any more than I would have admitted to my own unhappiness or the longing with which I recalled the other boy, whoever he had been. It was possible that I had imagined him—sometimes this seemed the most likely scenario—but there were nonetheless weeks and months of near-dreaming in which I believed him to be a kind of ghost, the spirit of a drummer boy fallen at Hubbardton two centuries before. Whatever the truth, he had rescued me from solitude and from fear and now the memory of him served to tether me to my receding childhood.

Perhaps, I considered, Lisa fulfilled a similar purpose in my father's life, though it's only now, as I write this, that I realize the extent to which she resembled my mother when she was young—in those days before my mother withdrew into herself so completely that she no longer remembered my name. "Go away, Charles," she told me, later that same summer, when I visited her for the final time in her apartment overlooking the East River. "Leave me in peace."

Charles. The name meant nothing to me, but I didn't correct her. I didn't say anything at all. Her hair was damp and matted, and she hadn't slept in days. The AC was switched off, despite the summer weather, and the windows were shut. Sweat had seeped through her nightgown. Her breasts were visible through the thin fabric.

Embarrassed, I backed out of the sitting room and made for the exit, leaving her there by the window with her face turned to the past. Sunlight poured through the parted curtains, scouring her features, but her eyes remained dark, unblinking.

≈≈

I went back to school. The baseball player had moved off campus, and I was assigned a new roommate, a second-year history major. He recommended that I transfer into his program, and I did. Unsurprisingly, I found myself drawn to the colonial period, so much so that I chose to write my third-year term paper on the strategic importance of the Saratoga campaign.

I spent the better part of the fall semester engaged in research. However, it quickly became apparent that the college's holdings were inadequate for my purposes, and I began to request materials from other universities and libraries.

The college reference librarian was an elderly man well past retirement age. He had worked at the library for nearly forty years and had long since ceased to take any interest in students' research. He filed his requests with robotic efficiency, asking no questions—not even when I asked him to acquire a complete list of British and Hessian casualties at Hubbardton.

Strictly speaking, this was not relevant to my research. But the past was close behind me, breathing in my ear, and I often woke from nightmares of mud and suffocating heat, the screams of the fallen or of those left behind. In these dreams I was running, always running, and always with the other boy beside me. He wore the uniform in which he had died, returning to rescue me while grown men around us played at war and slaughter. I couldn't speak of these fantasies to anyone, of course, though they continued to trouble me, even on waking, when I thought of ghosts, and the ways in which a spirit might pass through the veil as from the shadow of a long illness: my father's cancer, my mother's depression.

The call came one night in December, shortly after dinnertime. The casualty lists had come in. I donned my winter jacket and trekked across campus to the library. Snowfall whirled on the air, sifting down from a sky clouded over into near-opacity.

I collected the documents from the reference desk and sequestered myself inside my usual carrel. There I learned that a total of thirty-eight British soldiers had fallen at Hubbardton. A further 125 were wounded, though it was possible that some later succumbed to their injuries. I spent hours poring over lists of the dead before turning my attention to the wounded, scanning names and ages, looking for ghosts, as I had always done, though I found nothing. There were no drummer boys listed among the slain or the wounded.

The closing bell sounded. The lights dimmed and went out, and in that place of darkness, I pulled on my coat. Outside, the snow continued to fall. I buried my hands in my pockets and trudged back to the dorm. Snowflakes turned and tumbled on the brisk air, gathering like fireflies around the sodium lamps, swooping to fill my vision, to light the violet skies.

≈≈

For my senior thesis, I built upon the previous year's

research and examined the Saratoga campaign in greater detail. Naturally, this entailed a research trip to southern Vermont, and I drove westward through New Hampshire that October, listening to the radio at maximum volume as the hills flowered and burst into shades of scarlet and yellow.

Passing through the town of Bennington, I crossed the New York border and walked the length of the old Bennington battlefield, snapping hundreds of photographs throughout the course of a balmy, mulch-scented afternoon. The next morning, I re-crossed the state boundary and drove north along Route 7 toward Hubbardton.

The battlefield at Hubbardton was said to be one of the best preserved sites associated with the Revolutionary War, and it was plain enough that it had, in fact, changed very little. As it was, the battlefield consisted of a broad swath of hilly pastureland bisected by a ridge of shrubs and crumbling fieldstones. Woods encroached on the pasture to my left—birches yellow with their last leaves—and I passed beyond them into the ranks of beech and maple.

This is where I had walked as a child. I knew this and yet there was nothing familiar in the dead growth or mossy stillness, the black puddles with their floating leaves. The weather was turning cold. The breath steamed from my lungs while the trees swayed and shivered, naked in the falling dusk. I walked among them for an hour or more, feeling nothing, not even loss, as though something essential had passed from my life before I was aware of it.

I should never have returned to the battlefield. There were no ghosts, no lights beyond the trees. The day closed over me, bending the shadows together, sweeping me toward the dark. I quickened my pace and walked until I reached an expanse of waterlogged pasture.

The field was un-mowed since summertime, overgrown with brittle weeds that rustled where the wind churned amongst them, releasing the odors of leaf-rot and standing water, the sour taste of mud and decay. I took out my camera. I snapped a few photographs. The horizon dimmed behind me, losing color, grey and empty as the trees.

≈≈

I graduated in the spring. My job prospects in Maine were non-existent, but I couldn't bring myself to return to New York. The reasons for this are complicated. They always are, I suppose. I've mentioned my mother's depression, which had worsened in recent years, and she now resided in an assisted living home where she received around-the-clock care and attention. "She's sleeping better these days," my father told me, managing the words between gasping breaths. "It was difficult for her, being on her own."

And now he too was alone. His relationship with Lisa had ended some months before. He had broken it off—and rather suddenly, I gathered—though we did not speak of it, just as we never discussed his illness. After four years, the cancer had spread throughout his chest so that it pained him to speak. He used to phone me up in the small hours merely to listen to me prattle on about work or the weather or the books I was reading.

Once, near the end, we talked until dawn. The horizon lightened, white with fog, and the sun surfaced out of the east, branching from itself in wiry lines like an infection in the blood.

"Goodnight," he said. His breath hissed in the receiver, and he mumbled something else before hanging up. I can't be certain, but it sounded like, "the night is so long."

When the last days came, I went home to be with him and sat by the bedside as he passed. Lisa came to the wake. She embraced me warmly and rested her head against my shoulder, and it was clear that she bore my father no bitterness despite the abrupt manner in which he had ended things. My mother arrived at the burial in the company of a female social worker. This other woman ignored me, as did my mother, who gazed into the open grave with the same intensity with which she had once regarded the neighbours' pond.

The priest closed his prayer book. A jet passed overhead, deafeningly loud. My mother took fright and scrabbled at her companion's arm. The other woman smiled, gently, removed my mother's hand with a practiced tenderness, and led her back to the waiting minivan.

That night, I dreamt of the house in Hubbardton. Again I stood on the back porch and looked out over the neighbours' pasture, boulders thrusting from the sod. My mother sat next to me, silent and shawled. She rocked soundlessly while the crows circled overhead, as though they had caught from us the scent of death, a muddy stench like old graves opening.

I wanted to tell her something—I don't remember what—but she remained oblivious, un-listening with the pond in her eyes. The whites shimmered and blurred, stretching the iris, which changed shape before me, assuming the outline of an approaching figure. It was small and dark and faintly rippling, brown where the light fell across its featureless head.

A young child. A boy.

"Go away, Charles," she said, and I awoke.

≈≈

My father's lease terminated upon his death. Renovations were planned, and the owners allowed me one week to box up and remove his belongings. In truth, a single day would have sufficed, for my father left behind him a bare three rooms emptied of all clutter save for a bed, a desk, and a tall bookcase topped with framed prints by Schiele and Matisse.

I spent the best part of an afternoon sorting through his books, placing the majority in donation boxes destined for the library. I kept a few volumes for myself—novels, mostly, some old books of poetry—as well as a 1909 edition of Parkman's *Montcalm and Wolfe* that I was surprised to spot on the bottom shelf.

The book fell open in my hands. Evidently, my father had marked his place with an old Polaroid, which he had subsequently forgotten about. The photo showed me when I was a child. I stood in a green meadow with the woods looming behind me, three years old and dressed in the same wool coat and tricorn that I remembered. But I wasn't alone.

The other boy was next to me, dressed in yellow with a drum slung from his shoulder. He was slightly older than I was—seven or eight at a guess—and he grinned widely, displaying his missing front teeth. The resemblance between us was unmistakable.

My father had written a caption underneath the image. *Charles & Paul*, it read. *Hubbardton Battlefield. Hubbardton, VT. July 1986.*

I called Lisa.

There was no one else I could contact, no one else in whom my father might have confided. Understandably, she proved reluctant to talk about Charles, but I pressed her. "Please," I said, unable to hide the desperation in my voice. My palms were sweating, and the phone slipped in my hands like an eel. "Tell me what happened to him."

She exhaled. "Well," she said, speaking slowly. "He died."

I said nothing.

"Your mother never wanted you to know," she continued. "She blamed herself for it, for what happened. Your father thought it was cruel to hide it from you, but he went along with her, hoping it might pass, her denial. But it never did."

"How did he die?"

"He drowned. This happened in August, your father said, during your last summer in Vermont. 1986? You and Charles were catching toads near the neighbours' pond while your mother watched you from the porch. Charles knew better than to go into the water, but he must have seen something, your father thought, because he went out too far. He slipped and fell and he couldn't right himself."

"But my mother, she—"

"It was hot that day. 'Hellishly hot,' your father said. She had dozed off. Your father must have heard something, though, because he came running. He hauled out your brother, but it was too late. 'He was all brown,' he said. Charles had drowned in the mud. He was covered in leeches. His hands, his face... Your poor father."

I closed my eyes, recalling the stench of the pond, the screams of circling crows. I coughed, choking back the taste of bile.

"And me?" I asked. "Where was I during all this?"

"You were there," she said. "Though you were too young to understand what was happening. Your father found you at the water's edge, staring at the place where Charles had gone under. You were so quiet. You hadn't even cried out."

I thanked her for talking with me and wished her goodnight.

We hung up.

But I called her back a few minutes later to ask about the re-enactment. Had my father ever mentioned anything? I told her the little I remembered. Sunlight and smoke. The drummer boy, his yellow coat. His hand around mine as we sprinted across the field.

"Oh, yes," she said. "Your father told me all about it. Charles was quite a hero that day."

≈≈

I went back to Hubbardton. I obtained the address of our old house from the town clerk and sought out the current owners. A young woman greeted me at the door. I introduced myself and explained that I had lived there some years before. Hearing this, she welcomed me inside and gave me a tour of the interior, indicating places where her husband had torn out the floorboards or shored up the roof.

Afterward she showed me onto the back porch. This alone had not changed, though my mother's rocker had been replaced by a pair of Adirondack chairs, which faced each other from opposite sides of the deck. "Do you mind if I look around?" I asked.

"Take your time," she said. "I'm sure there's a lot you want to see."

My steps carried me downhill to the pond. The water was filthy, occluded with mud and algae. Sunlight pooled near the center, greasy and slick. Weeds thrust up from the crumbling margin, their roots exposed where the soil had sloughed away. The pond was expanding, swollen with rain and creeping outward.

Charles had seen something in the water. That's what

Lisa had said. But all I could see was the sky, appearing in reflection where the light bled away into the mire. Clouds were visible—wispy and ragged, adrift in the blackness—but there was no sign of life, or movement, or the muddy figure for whom my mother had watched and waited all those years ago.

She would have taken him in her arms, I knew. She would have begged for his forgiveness. And so she had kept herself awake, going without sleep for days at a stretch, forcing herself to relive the afternoon he had drowned. Eventually, she had retreated into madness, though he haunted her there as well, as he had also haunted me—and I recalled the figure from my dream, the way it had advanced on my mother, body rippling, black on brown. Leeches.

The silence was complete. An hour passed, but still the pond lay motionless. I stood and watched the water as my mother had done and thought of the life that had closed around me, snapping shut like a trap while Charles ran beyond, his yellow coat flying out behind.

He had slipped from memory into dreams and finally into absence, becoming "the other boy," the lack from which I had made a life. A ghost. For years I had longed to believe in such things but now the realization gave no comfort. It gave nothing at all but took from me as it had always done, leaving only fear and guilt and silence.

I kicked at the edge of the pond. Mud swirled in the stagnant water, welling up to blot out the reflected sky. For a moment, I could see the bottom, a moonscape of pebbles and drowned weeds. A white shape in the water. It turned on the waves I had created, disgorged from the murk and rising. Bones. The skeleton of a frog or toad. The pond settled, and it was gone.

The sky reappeared. The daylight faded, and I walked back to the car.

WIDDERSHINS

Lynda E. Rucker

I'm told there is a path, and a gate, and beyond it a spring, but so far I haven't been able to find any of it. I tried to find it yesterday and ended up in the forest. I keep ending up in the forest.

I came to this corner of Ireland to get away from myself, or find myself, I'm not sure which, after I crashed and burned my career and my family and everything that mattered to me back home in Oregon. If you've lived in Portland you've heard of the ad agency where I used to work, and if you've lived anywhere you've seen our—their—commercials, and yes, it ended badly, just like everything in what had, up to that point, been something of a charmed life. I was asked to leave my job not long after my wife left me for an airline pilot and moved to Toronto with our two daughters. Well, the daughters weren't *really* mine—they were hers from her first marriage—so I didn't have any say in where they went. But they *were* mine, too, I loved them like my own. So a year ago I was a successful, still young-ish guy with a prestigious career and a gorgeous family and today I'm an aging dude mucking around a part of Ireland even Irish people have barely heard of. Ch-ch-changes, as the song goes.

The light here, when there's light, is lovely. Mostly, it's dark and gloomy, which suits me.

Eoin was an old friend from college. That was a long

time ago. He'd gone back home to Ireland after he finished school in America, but we'd kept in touch off and on over the years. He and his partner Mary bought some property up here in the midlands where Mary's family originally came from. Right now they're up in the hills living out of their camper, breaking some preliminary ground on their unzoned and, I presume, illegal cob house. For the month of May, Eoin had offered me the run of the cottage they were renting. It's an old stone cottage—sounds romantic, but it's cold as death and the only heating comes from the coals I burn in the fireplace. Come in the spring, Eoin had said. The weather's best then. I don't know if that was some kind of Irish humour or what, but it's rained almost every day since I got here. The cold gets to me but the rain's not so bad, really, not that different from Portland. Luckily I like walking in the rain, so I go out every day looking for the gate. Eoin and Mary will be back down the mountain at the end of next week and if I haven't found it by then they can show me where it is.

The village isn't too far from me, a single street with a few shops down at one end and a row of more stone cottages at the top. Locally they're called the "railway cottages" because a railroad used to run behind them, though there's no trace of it now. It's said the inhabitants were so poor that the children would run out and steal coal off the train when it passed. Today the cottages are brightly painted and sport colourful window boxes. Two are rented out as holiday homes. People come here to fish and drive boats up and down the canal, probably more than ever since the Celtic Tiger died mid-leap. I think foreign holidays have fallen off the agenda for a lot of people these days.

In the village there are eight pubs, three butchers, a grocery, a produce place, a hardware store—everything you could need, really. Even a library, and Eoin's lent me his card.

I don't visit the village much, though. Mostly, I walk. It's good for thinking, and I used to make my living thinking, coming up with new ideas and new ways to get people to spend their money. So I keep imagining that I can think my way out of this hole I find myself in. And I look for the gate.

I don't know why I'm so obsessed with finding it. I heard about it the day after Eoin and Mary went up the mountain. I was in town to get a few groceries and I stopped in at one of the pubs and a farmer started chatting with me—people are friendly like that here, and not many tourists, foreign ones I mean, come through these parts, so they aren't sick of us. And the farmer said, oh, you're staying up near the old Kelly place and I said yes and then well, I don't know, because I didn't, and he said, aye, it's the old Kelly place.

If you go walking, he continued, there's a spring on the property, full of fish, if you can find it. He said, your man there can tell you all about it, and he pointed at the bartender who looked even older than the farmer and the bartender just looked at us and went back to whatever he was doing, talking to some guys at the other end of the bar and the farmer laughed and I felt like it was a joke everyone was in on but me.

You walk south, the farmer told me, and you'll come to a path. And you follow the path and you'll come to an old stone wall with a wooden gate built into it and you open the gate and pass through and you'll come to the spring and if you like fishing you'll find plenty of it.

Do I like fishing? I don't know. I did as a child. I don't know anything right now, though. I'm no longer the man I was. I don't know who I am anymore.

I said, Yes, I like fishing, and he said, oh, that's too bad, then.

WEDNESDAY NIGHT

It's the middle of the night. I haven't looked at the time because I know it would depress me. I woke from a nightmare, clawing at the duvet, and I can't fall asleep again, and it's so cold in here, too cold to get up and try to get a fire going. How can it be May? It's like the dead of winter. I thought I heard something on the roof of the cottage. It's probably nothing, or maybe it's the rooks, those noisy birds that scared me the first few mornings I heard them shrieking outside.

It's time to confess something I haven't even been able to confess to myself, but the middle of the night is when these things rise up and take you. I don't miss them. My wife Tanya, the children, Stephanie, who's ten, and her little sister Kimmie, seven. "My girls," I used to call them collectively, because that's the sort of thing you do. I ought to feel their absence like a great stinking pit inside of me, like a hurt that will never heal, but the truth is I miss what they represented and the life we made. I don't actually miss *them*, have trouble recalling their faces as I write this, and that probably is a clue as to why Tanya left me for the pilot. I miss the man I was when I had them in my life. The man with the beautiful wife, the beautiful daughters. This realization concerns me. Were they just interchangeable parts of me? I don't think so. I am not unfeeling. I had believed I'd loved Tanya and Stephanie and Kimmie deeply, but what I felt when I lost the job and the house and the family was most of all shame, embarrassment, a concern about what people would think of *me*.

I'm huddled here in bed, getting a cramp trying to write under the covers by flashlight (because it's so cold) and I am trying to make myself miss them to no avail. Maybe I'm traumatized. Emotionally numb. I'd seen a counselor a few times as it was all falling apart, when I still had a job that would pay for such things. He used words like that to describe it. *PTSD*, he said; not just for combat soldiers any longer! Apparently your wife leaving you for a pilot is traumatizing too. And that trauma leaves you out of touch with your feelings.

Or maybe I never had any feelings to begin with.

THURSDAY

I walked into town today, thinking I'd take a break from the search for the gate. I'm not really obsessed. I just don't have anything better to do.

I bought some coffee and some milk and eggs at the grocery store and put them in my backpack, and I stopped in at the pub again. The farmer was there.

"I see you haven't found the gate yet," he said.

I waved the bartender over and bought us both pints. "How'd you know?" I said.

The farmer laughed. "You wouldn't be here if you had."

A spike of anger surprised me. I can be a decent sport, but I guess wasn't in the mood to play the dumb American tourist today. "Let me guess," I said. "It's a gate to fairyland, and once I find it, and cross to the other side, I'll never be seen or heard from again."

The farmer put a hand on my arm. "Drink up, lad. I've a story to tell ye." I don't think anyone's ever called me a *lad* before. So I took a swallow of stout and I listened.

FRIDAY

I didn't feel like writing anymore yesterday. The farmer told such an unpleasant story that I didn't want to experience it again so soon; I went to bed early and couldn't sleep for hours, in my freezing bed looking out the open curtains at the cold overcast sky.

When I did sleep my dreams were wrong. I dreamed of figures that rose from the earth and rose from the trees and rose from stone and came down from the hills and gathered outside the cottage in a ring and sang at me in low and ancient and terrible voices.

It was the fault of the farmer, the nightmare. The old Kelly farm, he'd said. Up near you.

I said, I don't know.

Good for you, he said. Sure you want to know?

Know what?

He nodded deliberately. Back in the 1980s, he said, there was supposed to be a, a kind of dance party up there. They had a name for it.

A rave?

That was it, he said. And folks came from all over the place, and there were some lads that wandered up past the gate with some girls.

He said there were old famine cottages up that way, and from the way he described things, with lots of leering and innuendo, it sounded like they thought it was a good spot to smoke a little hash and fuck the girls. Place was

111

deserted then, too. Owner fucked off to America decades ago. Or maybe England. Who knows? Gone, anyway.

Had they talked to anyone local, the farmer said, they'd have been warned away. They'd have been told not to go through the forest and past the gate. If only they'd bothered to ask.

The farmer leaned in close to me. "They found them," he said, "or what was left of them." Only then did I notice his bad breath, and the ring of rotted teeth remaining in his mouth. He made some sounds that I realized were laughter. "What was left was their heads, and some arms. They were in the forest. The parts that were left were hung from trees in the forest. What was done to the girls was even worse."

I said, "Oh, God."

"It got out," he said. "What was in got out for a little while but people drove it back behind the gate."

I noticed then that the others all sat together, and away from him. It occurred to me that maybe that was because they didn't like him. I don't like him much, either. I took a sip of my stout and it was foul, as though his story had turned it rancid.

"It's true," the farmer said in the direction the bartender, "isn't it?"

The bartender looked down our way and made a gesture with his head in which I could have read either agreement or dissent. I didn't wait around to learn any more. I shoved the drink away and stumbled out the door. I thought I heard laughter behind me, though I couldn't be sure, and all I wanted was to get away.

MONDAY

I spent the rest of Friday convincing myself they were fucking with me.

There was no path. There was no forest. There was no gate. Certainly, there were no entrails and soft bits of flesh strung from trees.

Friday night I did something new: I walked back into the village, looking for something to do. I ended up in a noisy kind of nightclub at the local hotel. Countless pints later I'd made a number of new friends, including

Catriona and Gerry and Declan. The three proved to be adept at prying my life story out of me, or as much as you can while shouting over the beats of aggressive dance music. I said I'd blown my career and Gerry said it sounded like my wife was blowing something else and I laughed with them; did that mean, I wondered, that I was getting better? Or maybe just drunker.

They knew all about the gate, or claimed they did. Who the hell knows anymore? I can't tell when these people are pulling my leg and when they're being sincere. I'm not sure they can, either.

"Ah, the gate!" Catriona shouted. She was quite drunk at this point, blonde hair tumbling over in her red face as she leaned in toward me, vodka-and-something sloshing from the top of her glass. "'Twas a witch that built it!"

"No, a druid I heard," Gerry said. "It's built from a what-do-you-call-it, a grove. Trees from a sacred druid grove. And when it starts to rot people go up there and rebuild it again."

"Who?" Catriona yelled. "What people?"

"I don't know!" Gerry shouted back, and they both dissolved into drunken laughter.

"I don't know any druids," Catriona shrieked, "do you?" and they were off again.

"It's a load of shite is what it is," Declan snapped. "It's a fuckin' gate built by a fuckin' farmer to keep his fuckin' sheep from running away. Wasn't never no fuckin' ravers murdered up there or witches or druids or curses or fuckin' leprechauns either." He stalked out after that with a cigarette in his hand. I found him sheltering from the pouring rain under the awning outside, smoking moodily.

I said, "Look, if I offended you back there…"

Declan spun on me. His eyes were wide. "Offended me. Offended me? If I offended you, he says!" He imitated my voice, my accent. "Stupid fucking blow-ins. Stupid fucking Americans. With your stupid fucking ideas about shamrocks and bombs and fucking charming little Irish people and what the fuck was that? *Druids*?"

I said, "But I never said anything about druids. That was the others," and by the look he gave me I knew I'd missed his point but I was too drunk to figure out how. He threw down his cigarette, pushed past me and was off up the road.

I went back in to join Catriona and Gerry and at first I thought they'd taken off, but finally spotted them making out in a corner. I left the nightclub with the dry stale taste of alcohol still on my tongue and the hangover already kicking in.

Going home in the dark was more difficult than I'd imagined it would be. No moon in the sky, and I kept stumbling over my own feet. Every once in a while a car would careen past me.

Naturally, this seemed like the best time imaginable to go looking for the gate.

And so rather than tucking myself into the freezing bed to shiver until dawn, I went looking for the path. I have never known a night so dark, and yet somehow I found the path immediately. Far in the distance I could hear something calling, maybe an owl, I don't know. It scared me so I started singing. I can't remember what I sang. I can't remember how I got to the gate.

Well, first I was in the forest, as always. The path before me narrowed as it always did and the trees closed in. And then I stumbled from the dark tunnel of trees and the moon passed from behind the clouds and spilled light all over the land and there it was, a wooden gate, closed, and on either side of it those stone walls you see all over Ireland. Beyond it, some crumbling stone cottages.

I put my hand on the gate. I felt the weight of its age.

I hesitated for just a moment before passing through. I hadn't really been joking when I said to the farmer that it was the gate to fairyland. I was afraid if I walked through it I'd be changed somehow. But wasn't I already changed? Hadn't I already walked through that metaphorical gate of life? Jesus—or *Jaysus*, as they say in these parts—I'd clearly had too much to drink, coming up with stupid shit like that.

I pushed on the gate. It resisted, and I realized I needed to lift it a little using both hands. And then it swung open before me. It was just an ordinary gate, and the other side was ordinary too.

I walked about a little bit. I poked around the derelict

cottages. The floors were muck. You could get stuck in them. I couldn't imagine anyone thinking going up there to get laid was a good idea, not unless you had a fetish for freezing mud. If anything gave lie to the farmer's tale it was that. The whole place altogether depressed me. I wondered why I'd been so anxious to find my way there in the first place.

Still, I wanted to find the stream as well, to see if it was all truly as the farmer had described it, so I made a wide circle round the cottages and headed downhill. I could hear the water running before I found it. I can't say if it was stocked with fish as the farmer had claimed—the moonlight glistened on the surface but didn't penetrate— but what surprised me was the discovery that someone had been there recently, several someones by the look of things. A circle of stones like seats ringed the remains of a fire, and tent pegs lay scattered nearby.

I stepped closer, and saw that where the moonlight fell, one of the trees had been scarred by carvings, mostly names and crudely drawn stick figures but one unfamiliar word as well: *tuaithbel.*

As I traced the outline of the letters with a finger, I heard something rustling nearby. I turned and saw it watching me from some brush. It was something—well, it was a fox. It must have been a fox. Its mouth opened; I'd have sworn it was struggling to summon some awful parody of human speech at me. Its tongue was very long and very red.

I hadn't realized they have such sharp, cunning faces.

TUESDAY

I don't know how I made it home that night, and I don't remember the rest of the weekend. But every morning I've woken with that word on my tongue: *tuaithbel,* along with a hollowed-out sense that pieces of my dreams were stolen from me while I slept.

Yesterday I walked back into town to use the library's internet service. It was drizzling and by the time I arrived I was wet and even colder than usual. I couldn't bring myself to ask the librarians about the murder—it seemed too vulgar, if a lie, and too raw and horrible if true. I tried a variety of search terms and found nothing at all. It's unlikely that such a bizarre event would have faded into obscurity.

Tuaithbel yielded more answers. I scanned the first page of results without clicking on any of them. "Against the sun," one snippet from an Irish dictionary explained, and from another, "lefthand, anti-clockwise, widdershins. To curse someone go *tuaithbel*." The rest of the results on the page were in Irish.

Widdershins. I had a vague memory of once doing a campaign for a small clothing company bearing the name; I knew the word without bothering to know what it meant and I'm sure they didn't really know either. They probably just thought it was a cool word. I googled that, too. *To go counter-clockwise. Bad luck. Opposite the sun's direction.* I'd have advised them to choose a different name, had I realized.

I sat back in my chair, rubbing my eyes and trying to remember in what direction I'd walked round the cottages. Had I gone *tuaithbel?* Did it matter?

With the librarian's help, I found a book that included some information on sacred trees. I read about the magical properties of oak and ash and hawthorn. I wondered what ancient people had discovered something terrible in that place and how they'd built the gate to keep it on the other side. Maybe ever since, people had kept rebuilding even though they no longer knew why, just like the fertility of hares accompanies Easter, and Christmas brings celebrations of light against a darkness no one believes in any longer.

Maybe it hadn't been the famine at all that drove people from the derelict cottages. Maybe it had been something else entirely.

I needed a drink.

I need one now. I know there is something at the window, looking in at me. It hides when I turn my head but it leaves its shape behind on the glass to frighten me. Its shape is a wrongness. All about the cottage is the smell of something that has been old and lost for far too long.

TUESDAY. LATER.

I went outside but I could hardly see a thing. Something rustled in a hedge. It turned out to be a fox. Just an ordinary one this time.

I'm very frightened. I came back in, and I've found someone has been in the house. Someone took pieces of coal and wrote that word all over the walls. *Tuaithbel.* Who would have done such a thing? I wasn't even out that long. Well, I don't think I so. Perhaps I was. Perhaps.

My own hands are so thick with coal dust. It's smearing this paper as I write. I can barely see the words now even as I set them down. It's because I was trying to rub out the words on the wall with my hands. I didn't put them there myself. I wouldn't do that.

After I left the library today, I went back to the pub. I took my usual spot at the bar. The farmer, for once, was nowhere to be seen. The bartender came over to me, his face as expressionless as ever.

"Where's . . . ?" I made a gesture toward the farmer's usual spot.

The bartender just looked at me. "I don't know who ye mean," he said.

I got angry. "The guy!" My voice was too loud and sounded very flat and very American to me. The men at the other end of the bar were staring. "The guy I talked to here!"

The bartender said, "You should leave."

"You know who I mean!"

The others were all older and smaller than me, respectable-looking in neat but worn sweaters and honest soiled hands. They weren't getting up from their stools yet, but they were wary, and had the look of men who knew how to handle themselves if needed. I can take a hint. I left.

TUESDAY. LATER STILL.

I am remembering now something Mary said to me off-handedly when I first got here. I'd forgotten it, the way you do, because it didn't matter at the time. They'd got the place very cheap, she said. There'd been a farm here and then the farmer up and left decades ago, seemingly overnight. And the place had been abandoned ever since.

"It was weird," Eoin said, hearing our conversation as he was coming in from outside and stomping the mud off his wellies. "Sure, people emigrated all the time, but not old country farmers, and not suddenly, and not for a reason like that."

"What was the reason?" I asked.

Mary said, "My mam remembered when it happened. It was said because of something he found in the earth, while tilling his fields. Something that upset him so that he went away forever."

"Something? What kind of something?"

"He wouldn't say," Mary told me. "He said it wasn't made of metal and it wasn't made of stone and it wasn't anything he could recognize. At first he took it out of the earth and brought it into the cottage. He thought it might be something historical, you know, something valuable. He said the night that he brought it into the cottage he passed the most terrible night of his life. That was all he would ever say about it, except that he buried it back again where he found it."

And then the roast was ready so we took it out and Eoin poured the wine and we all forgot about the farmer and his find.

I should have remembered that. I should not have sought the gate.

WEDNESDAY

Dawn comes early here. It's Wednesday morning that still feels like an endless Tuesday because I never slept. Just past daybreak, and it's going to be a rare clear morning as evidenced by the soft blues and sunrise pastels smearing the sky. I'm writing this in the back garden, propping my notebook on the little stone wall that encircles it. The air is crisp and clean and everything feels new. The light is magical. It's the kind of day you'd wake to and know whatever you'd faced up to that point, and no matter what happened, everything was about to be okay.

It is the kind of morning that makes up for everything. It makes up for all the pain of being alive. It is the kind of morning so beautiful that it is enough.

And that matters, because it may be the last morning for me.

Rather than sleeping, I had dreamed with my eyes open and my senses about me. I had dreamed about something a young Earth made wrong, something that then hid itself *in* the Earth, and found itself trapped. I dreamed about something that could sleep for a very long time and wake hungry. Always hungry.

I dreamed about people who would design rituals and protocols to ensnare it, or imagine they had done so. Who can say that it mattered which way I walked round the cottages. Who can say whether the oak and the ash and the hawthorn made any difference. In the end, we all find ourselves in the same place.

Sooner or later we all go widdershins.

Whatever it is that I unleashed the night I found the gate, it's been driven back before, so it can happen again. I don't really know how it's done. I doubt anybody does anymore. But I'm so hollowed out I imagine that if there is any old knowledge left to fill anyone when the time comes that it can fill me, that I can act as a sort of vessel for whatever protection was left there long ago by wiser folk. It's no great loss to anyone if I don't return.

I am leaving this book behind just in case. I don't know in case of what. I don't know if it will do any good. I don't know that anyone would or could believe anything that I've written here. Soon it won't matter. Soon it will all have ended, or it will not have.

I have never been a courageous man and I am not now. But the last waking dream I had was of a different Earth, of an Earth that might have been, or maybe an Earth that was or is or will be. An Earth that belonged to *them*. A braver man would not risk the stringing of his own beloved skins and soft organs through the indifferent trees. A braver man would take his chances and flee.

But they have the measure of my soul already. I am sure of it. And so I will attempt to walk them back through the gate, walk them widdershins, walk them *tuaithbel*, walk them back into the never-was that ought to never be. If I am lucky, which I used to be and am not any longer, I might save myself in the process, remaking myself, becoming whole again.

If only I can find my way back.

Back through the gate, and out of the forest, and walking with the sun.

CONTRIBUTORS

Ray Cluley's stories have appeared in various dark places, such as *Black Static* and *Interzone* from TTA Press, *Not One of Us,* and the *Darker Minds* anthology from Dark Minds Press. He has a story forthcoming in *Crimewave,* also TTA Press, and another in the Edgar Allan Poe anthology, *Where Thy Dark Eye Glances,* from Lethe Press. A novelette with Spectral Press is due in 2014. His work has been selected by Ellen Datlow for her *Best Horror of the Year* anthology, translated into French for *Ténèbres,* and this year 'Night Fishing' from issue 3 of *Shadows & Tall Trees,* was selected by Steve Berman for *Wilde Stories 2013.* Ray also writes non-fiction, but generally he prefers to make stuff up. You can find out more at probablymonsters.wordpress.com

Gary Fry's recent books are *Conjure House, Emergence* (both published by DarkFuse), and *Shades of Nothingness* (PS Publishing). Ramsey Campbell has called him a master of psychological horror. He runs Gray Friar Press, one of the U.K.'s most respected genre publishers. Gary can be found online here: www.gary-fry.com

Richard Gavin is widely regarded as a master of numinous horror fiction in the tradition of Arthur Machen, Algernon Blackwood, and H.P. Lovecraft. His work has appeared in *The Best Horror of the Year, The Magazine of Fantasy & Science Fiction,* and the *Black Wings* anthologies. His books include *Charnel Wine, Omens, The Darkly Splendid Realm,* and *At Fear's Altar.*

S.T. Joshi calls Richard Gavin "one of the bright new stars of contemporary weird fiction." Richard has also published horror criticism and essays on primordial occultism. His column 'Echoes from Hades' can be found on the acclaimed website *The Teeming Brain*. He lives in Ontario, Canada with his beloved wife and their children.

Eric Lacombe is a visual artist based in Lyon, France. His work has been exhibited at Lazarew Gallery in Paris, and he is represented by HK Art Agency. You can find him online at: monstror.blogspot.com

V. H. Leslie is an English lecturer, who teaches in a college in Hampshire, England. Previous stories have appeared in *Black Static*. She also writes academic pieces, focusing on nineteenth-century literature. She recently completed a novel.

Claire Massey's short stories have been published in *Best British Short Stories*, *Murmurations: An Anthology of Uncanny Stories About Birds*, *A cappella Zoo*, *Unsettling Wonder* and elsewhere. Two of her stories are available as chapbooks from Nightjar Press, of which one—"Into the Penny Arcade"—appears in *The Best Horror of the Year Volume 5*. Claire lives in Lancashire, England, with her two young sons.

Daniel Mills is the author of *Revenants: A Dream of New England* (Chomu Press, 2011) and the novella *Unhallowed Ground* (DarkFuse, 2012). His short fiction has appeared in various journals and anthologies, including *Black Static*, *A Season in Carcosa*, *Fungi*, and *The Mammoth Book of Best New Horror 23*. He lives in Vermont.

Lynda E. Rucker's fiction has appeared in such places as *F&SF*, *Black Static*, *The Mammoth Book of Best New Horror*, and *The Year's Best Dark Fantasy and Horror*, and she has stories forthcoming in *Nightmare Magazine*, *Postscripts*, and the British Fantasy Society anthology *The Burning Circus*. Her first collection, *The Moon Will Look Strange*, is due out from Karōshi Books in June.

Karin Tidbeck lives in Malmö, Sweden, and writes in Swedish and English. Her stories have appeared in Weird Tales, Shimmer, Strange Horizons and the anthologies

Odd? and *Steampunk Revolution.* She has published a story collection and a novel in Swedish; her debut collection in English, *Jagannath,* won the William L Crawford Award 2013 and was shortlisted for the Tiptree Award 2012. She blogs at www.karintidbeck.com

D.P. Watt is a writer living in the bowels of England. He balances his time between lecturing in drama and devising new 'creative recipes', 'illegal' and 'heretical' methods to resurrect a world of awful literary wonder. His short stories have appeared with Side Real Press, Megazanthus Press, Hieroglyphic Press, Gray Friar Press and his two novellas, *The Ten Dictates of Alfred Tesseller* and *Dehiscence* are available from Ex Occidente Press. His collection *An Emporium of Automata* was reprinted in 2013 by Eibonvale Press. You can find him at: www.theinterludehouse.com

Praise for *Shadows & Tall Trees*

"Michael Kelly's Shadows and Tall Trees is a smart, soulful, illuminating investigation of the many forms and tactics available to those writers involved in one of our moment's most interesting and necessary projects, that of opening up horror literature to every sort of formal interrogation. It is a beautiful and courageous journal."
  —Peter Straub, Best-Selling Author of *Ghost Story*, and *A Dark Matter*

" ...elegant digest-sized format and consistently good supernatural, ghost, and weird fiction...This looks to be the perfect magazine for aficionados of low-key horror. Bravo!"
  —Ellen Datlow, *The Best Horror of the Year 3*

"Like mist creeping though a northern forest, this journal of the ghostly and ghastly will have you starting at sudden noises, and recoiling from half-glimpsed faces in the shadows on the wall."
  —Laird Barron, Author of *The Croning*, and *Occultation*

"Shadows and Tall Trees comes on like the wendigo, or a will-o'-the-wisp, consistently quiet and ominous and delicious and very welcome indeed."
  —Glen Hirshberg, Author of *The Book of Bunk*, and *Motherless Child*

"Shadows & Tall Trees is a really strong collection of stories, a high quality product with high quality writing. I thoroughly recommend it."
—Anthony Watson, Dark Musings

"Just received a copy of the latest issue of this superb little publication from Undertow Books. The editor, Michael Kelly, is creating something quite special here, I feel. Expertly produced and presented, an example of what a horror publication of this type should 'feel' like when you pull it out of the envelope. Another great selection of tight, quiet horror stories in this issue, stories that unsettle and cause the reader to think beyond the parameters of the ordinary. Issue 2 contained a story 'Back Amongst the Shy Trees' by Steve Rasnic Tem that any writer of horror ought to aspire to.
—Danny Rhodes, The Crow's Nest II

"Editor/publisher Michael Kelly's aim, is, professedly, to offer good quality short fiction in the horror genre. I can testify that he's doing a great job and the third issue of Shadows & Tall Trees provides further evidence of his continuous success in that difficult task. The journal (which actually has the format and the layout of a short story anthology) manages once again to recruit excellent writers at the top of their game. I guarantee it's worth your money."
—Mario Guslandi, Horror World

"Shadows and Tall Trees appears to have a bright future and may well become one of the places to go to find new weird fiction."
—Speculative Fiction Junkie

"Kelly is doing a wonderful job collecting and publishing authors who really have significant literary talents."
—Benjamin Uminsky, Goodreads

Shadows & Tall Trees is the flagship publication of Undertow Publications (UP), an independent publisher based near Toronto, Canada.

Enquiries can be made by regular post or e-mail, and should be addressed to the editor at:

Shadows & Tall Trees
c/o Michael Kelly, Editor
1905 Faylee Crescent
Pickering, ON
L1V 2T3
Canada

undertowbooks@gmail.com

www.undertowbooks.com

CPSIA information can be obtained
at www.ICGtesting.com
Printed in the USA
LVOW12s0624010917
547231LV00001B/43/P